MAGIC WAND RANCH

A PARANORMAL ROMANTIC COMEDY

CAROLINE MICKELSON

BON ACCORD PRESS

Magic Wand Ranch

by Caroline Mickelson

Copyright © 2015 Caroline Mickelson

1

Fiona Cantrell twirled around in front of a full length mirror, admiring the red sequined gown that she'd just conjured up. She cocked her head to the side. As dazzling as it was, and as well as the color complimented her fair skin and chestnut brown hair, the sequins might be a bit much. At least for daytime wear. Packing for her new life in London was proving to be far more tricky than she'd imagined.

She reached for her magic wand and, with a delicate flick of the wrist, sent a flutter of gold sparkles swirling around her. When they settled, she studied her reflection critically. No, a navy power suit went a tad too far in the opposite direction. She sighed. "I wish someone was here to help me decide."

"Will I do?"

Startled, Fiona whirled around, her eyes searching for the person who'd just spoke. "Who's there?"

"Your boss." A male form materialized. "Sorry to startle you."

Relieved to see a friendly face, Fiona smiled warmly. "Hello, Liam." She leaned in and kissed his cheek. "Are you here as my boss or as my fairy godfather?"

Liam Kennedy, dressed in his uniform of faded Levi's and white t-shirt, slipped his hands in his back pockets and leaned against the wall. "A bit of both, you could say."

Fiona scooped up a pile of clothing from a chair and dropped it into the open suitcase on her bed. "Have a seat. I was just deciding what to pack."

"So I see." Liam surveyed her room. It looked like a ladies clothing boutique ten minutes after a tornado had torn through it. "Can we take a walk? I need to talk to you."

Fiona's eyes widened slightly. Something in his voice sounded different. Serious. "Of course, let me just change." With a quick flick of her wand, she exchanged the business suit for a gray track suit and a pair of aqua walking shoes. She led her boss through the maze of moving boxes that filled every available square inch of floor space in her condo. Once they were outside, she fell into step beside him. "What's so important that you interrupted your honeymoon to drop in on me?"

Liam's wide grin answered her unspoken question. There wasn't trouble in paradise yet. But if Liam was so besotted with his new witch of a wife, what was he doing here with such a pensive expression on his face?

They crossed the street and headed along the trail that led to a large duck pond. Towering trees provided ample shade, and a light breeze blew through the afternoon air. Fiona inhaled. The weather was simply gorgeous. She was going to miss the bright blue skies when she arrived in England. A vision of herself walking through London in a gray wool coat with a splashy red umbrella sent a thrill through her. Her new promotion as chief liaison to the United Paranormal Council's European division was an absolute dream come true. Simply put, she was the luckiest fairy godmother alive. Life just couldn't get any better than this.

"Fiona, there's a problem."

Fiona's feet quit moving and she reached out to grab a hold of Liam's arm. "What kind of problem?" She searched his eyes for an answer but couldn't read his expression. She'd known Liam for years. He not only made for a wonderful boss but, as cliché as it sounded, he was the older brother she would have loved to have had. There wasn't a single thing about him that she didn't either adore or respect, except for his new wife, Tessa. The woman was a witch. Literally. Fiona's mind raced. Did this have something to do with her new job?

She sucked in her breath. "Tessa wants her job back, doesn't she?"

"This isn't about my wife."

But Fiona was in no mood to hear him sing Tessa's praises. "I knew it. I told you, didn't I, Liam? I told you that she wouldn't be happy unless she had-" but the rest of her sentence came out as a mumbled, unintelligible, and very garbled sentence. Her hands flew to her throat, her eyes widened. Oh, no, Liam did not just do that to her. She stomped her foot in silent protest.

Liam held up his hands. "I'm sorry, Fiona. I really am. But when you get on the subject of my wife, it's hard to get you back on track. Will you hear me out?"

Fiona narrowed her eyes. She'd love to give Liam Kennedy an earful but this wasn't the right time or right place. Begrudgingly, she nodded her agreement.

With a quick glance around to make sure they weren't being observed, Liam tossed a pinch of gold glitter at her.

"Don't ever do that again. Otherwise I will have to cross you off my list of very favorite people." She drew in a deep breath and then another. Once fortified with fresh air, she began to walk. It was no surprise to her when Liam fell into step beside her. She looked sideways at him. "In return, I won't say a word about your wife ever again. Deal?"

Liam smiled gratefully. "You're a gem, Fiona. I'm going to miss you terribly when you're gone."

That sounded hopeful. "So, you're not pulling me from the assignment?"

Liam shook his head. "That's not why I'm here. Not exactly, anyway."

"Good, because I want this job more than I've ever wanted anything in my life." How to put this into words? "I mean, London, Liam. Just think of it. Me, Fiona Cantrell, living in England." She laughed aloud. "It's a dream come true." And she owed a great deal of the credit for her promotion to Liam, and indirectly to his wife. Both Liam and Tessa had been up for the same job but they'd fallen in love, which complicated everything. For them. Not for her. They'd ended up married and she'd ended up with the opportunity of a lifetime. A win-win if ever one existed. "I can hardly wait to leave."

"Well, you're going to have to wait."

She stopped walking. Again. "What did you just say?"

Liam tucked her arm in his. "Let's walk. We're not burning calories when we're standing still."

Despite her worry at the turn in the conversation, she couldn't help but smile. Liam Kennedy was the epitome of good health, right down to his last sculpted muscle. Fiona, however, could best be described as curvaceous. She was fit though, and the fact she sounded slightly out of breath was due more to her state of confusion more than her lack of fitness. "I'll walk, you talk."

Liam shot her an appreciative glance. "I've always thought of you as the ultimate team player. Which is why I didn't hesitate to recommend you for the job in London. We both know it's a huge career leap but I know you can handle it. But first I need your help with one more thing before you leave."

"Is that all? Of course, I'll help you. I have three days before I'm due in London. Why the heck didn't you just ask me straight out?"

"I'm getting to that part. What I want you to do is going to take more than three days. It's likely to take up all of the time you were going to tour Britain, so if you can complete this assignment, you'll be getting to London just before your new job starts."

Fiona thought as they walked on in silence for several minutes. If anyone other than Liam were asking, the easy answer would be an emphatic 'no'. Her itinerary was set, as so was her mind. But she owed so much of her career success to him, not to mention this entire opportunity. She turned to look at him. "Do you remember what an absolute nightmare I was on my first assignment?"

He laughed. "You mean the great glitter storm of 2008? I remember it well. But no one stayed in the hospital for more than a day or two, so all ended well."

"Very funny. But seriously, you were a great teacher and I couldn't have had a better boss. So, whatever I can do to help you, I will." And she'd do it quickly too so she could sneak in a few extra days of sight-seeing and shopping before her first day on the job. "When do I start?"

Liam guided her toward a park bench and they sat facing each other. "I think the question you should be asking is 'where am I going?'.

Fiona waved her hands. "Enough with the cryptic speech, Liam. I said I'd help you, so just tell me what it is that you need."

"Do you remember meeting a woman named Bethany when we visited Tessa at the spa?"

"I do. She was the young mother whose husband is serving in Afghanistan, right?"

Liam nodded. "That's her. She'd doing a great job getting in shape but ideally she should really stay there for several more weeks. Tessa thinks-"

Fiona managed to stifle a groan. She'd known all along that this would somehow lead back to Tessa, which left her unsettled, and more than a little suspicious.

"-that Bethany might leave earlier than she should because she's concerned about her kids," Liam continued. "So we thought-"

Translation, Tessa thought....

"-that if there was someone to help watch the kids then-"

"You want me to babysit?" Fiona shot to her feet. "That's the important task you want me to give up time in Europe for? Really?"

"Please sit, Fiona." Liam patted the seat beside him. He waited until she sank back down before he spoke. "I need someone who is completely trustworthy. Someone who is endlessly good-hearted and who can think on her feet."

"You need Mary Poppins."

"She was busy." He grinned. "But you were my second choice."

Fiona didn't even try to hide her smile. "Oh, for heaven's sake, I'll do it." Why not help out? She didn't have much experience with kids. Okay, none actually, but how hard could it be? Especially if she let her magic wand do the hard work? Nap time? A pinch of gold glitter worked as well as a sleeping pill. Homework she couldn't help with? Her magic wand could procure straight A's in short order. "Consider it my thank you for all the times you've been so good to me."

Liam pulled her to her feet and gave her a quick hug. "I am deeply grateful. Bethany will be too." He reached into his back pocket and pulled out a folded sheet of paper. "All the details are here, and if you can leave tomorrow, that would be perfect."

"What kind of clothes will I need?"

"We're back to that, are we? Not the red sequins, that's for sure." He pointed to the piece of paper. "Everything you need to know is in there, except for one little, tiny thing." He looked over her shoulder as if he'd just spotted a fascinating leaf on the tree just behind her. "It's hardly worth mentioning."

She snapped her fingers to reclaim his attention. "There's a catch?"

He shook his head. "Not exactly."

"Spit it out, Kennedy."

He laid a hand on her shoulder. "You can't use your magic. No wand. No glitter."

And then he was gone. Just like that.

Incredulous, Fiona spun around. "Liam?" But she was alone in the park with only a curious squirrel staring at her. No magic? Why on earth would Liam go to all the trouble of arranging for a fairy godmother for Bethany's kids and then tell her she couldn't use her magic? He couldn't be serious. No. That last bit had to be a joke, albeit a stupid one. Most likely it had been Tessa's idea. The woman had no sense of humor.

Just to be sure, Fiona reached into her track suit pockets but her wand was gone. She plopped down on the bench and stared at the squirrel for a long moment. As if to offer sympathy, it scampered a bit closer to her. "Don't worry," Fiona reassured it. "I have an extra wand and a secret stash of glitter at home. I've got this covered."

2

Cody Proctor was a man who knew a thing or two about fear. He'd spent half of his life on the rodeo circuit, which gave him a full fourteen years of adrenaline-packed experiences to prepare him for this very moment. But fighting to stay on the back of a bucking bronco for eight full seconds suddenly seemed like a Sunday school cake walk compared to the two fierce opponents who blocked his path.

"We had hot dogs last night." Mitchell, his six-year-old nephew, fixed his hands squarely on his hips. Clearly the boy meant business. "And the night before that too."

Uncertain as to quite what point the boy

was trying to make, Cody glanced at his other nephew. But five-year-old Brian's expression was as stoic as his brother's and held no clue as to what Cody's next move should be. It was an old-fashioned stand-off, pure and simple. "But your mom told me that you liked hot dogs."

The boys exchanged a quick glance that Cody couldn't decipher. He took off his hat and ran his fingers through his hair. When he'd initially agreed to watch his sister Bethany's two sons for a few weeks so she could go off to a health spa, he'd never imagined he'd end up in so far over his head. The first thing Cody had done was outfit the boys in Wrangler jeans, Roper shirts, boots, and cowboy hats. Duly outfitted, they'd settled into life on the ranch and had happily played with the dogs, fed the chickens, and practically tied themselves up in knots trying to learn how to rope a barrel. They'd gamely eaten macaroni and cheese, chicken nuggets, and hot dogs. Over and over again. But now it was clear to see that the thrill was wearing off.

"We used to like hot dogs," Mitchell said. "But we're over them."

Brian crossed his arms over his chest. "Over," he echoed.

If his sister had been on the receiving end of this conversation, Cody would have just laughed. Being an uncle was fun and games, hugs and high fives, and he loved it. But being the boys' caregiver was a whole 'nother rodeo. Between answering a quarter million questions a day, watching the piles of laundry grow, and trying to keep those little tummies filled, Cody had a new appreciation for his sister. As a military wife, Bethany kept her household running while her husband was deployed. The least he could do was keep things together until she got back. "I've got this dinner thing covered. Let's head to Maude's Diner for a burger."

Mitchell frowned. "Is that the place with the green mashed potatoes?"

"They're not green. The lighting is just funny in there." Cody reached out to ruffle his nephew's mop of curls. "Now go get your boots on, both of you, and meet me out by the truck."

CODY SLIPPED a Garth Brooks CD into the player and turned the volume up as he headed out onto the highway. He wore a smile for much of the twenty minute drive as he listened to his nephews attempt to sing along. They didn't do too poor a job considering they only knew about half the words.

Maude's parking lot was less than half full. Cody swung the truck into an empty spot and held the door open for the boys. As they hopped out, he marveled at their resilient little spirits. Their father had been overseas for months, their mother had been gone for weeks, which, to Cody's way of thinking, gave them full whining rights. But both boys were living in the moment and making the best of things. He'd do well to remember that in the week ahead.

"Hey, Cody," a middle-aged waitress greeted him when they entered. "I see your handsome little cowboys are still with you." She grabbed a couple of kids menus and a small bucket of crayons. "Follow me."

Cody took off his hat and slid into the booth across from his nephews. After exchanging a bit of small talk with the waitress, he ordered three bottles of root beer. "Okay, boys, can you please tell Miss Sara what you'd like to eat?"

Mitchell ordered first. "I'd like a hot dog, please."

Brian nodded in agreement. "Me too, and I'd like some mashed potatoes with mine."

Cody didn't try to hide his amusement. "Funny thing is, we just had a drawn out discussion back at the house about these little guys being tired of hot dogs," he told the waitress. "I guess they're just tired of the way I make them."

She laughed. "Sounds about right. Let me go get those root beers for y'all."

After a spirited word search game, Cody drew out his cell phone and pulled up the calendar app. He did a quick count. If he was hitched up and got on the road to Tucson within the next couple of days, he should be fine. The annual Fiesta de los Vaqueros rodeo was the first outdoor event on the pro-rodeo calendar and one he really enjoyed. Between the Arizona sunshine and the enthusiastic crowds, it was a great way to kick off the season. There was also the not-so-little matter of prize money and a lucrative endorsement deal if he pulled off a win. He was looking forward to the challenge.

Just as he was about to slip the phone back in his pocket, it rang. A quick glance at screen told him it was his sister. His eyebrows rose. Bethany wasn't much for talking on the phone, she usually preferred texts. "Hey sis, what's up?"

"Hi Cody. How are the boys?"

He glanced across the table. Mitchell and Brian were in the middle of a full out tug-of-war over an orange crayon. "They're great," he assured his sister. "Little angels." Several long seconds of silence told him that this wasn't just a call to check up on the kids. "What's wrong?"

She sighed. "I don't know what to do."

"Hang on a sec," he held the phone aside and snapped his fingers to get his nephews attention. "Guys, I'm going to talk to your mom for a minute. I want you to behave yourselves, got it?" He held out his hand and nodded to the orange crayon. "Fork it over."

Brian handed him the much sought after orange crayon.

"Good job, guys. Now please just color quietly for a moment." Satisfied they were done squabbling, he went to the back of the diner where he could still see the boys but they couldn't overhear his conversation just in case it was bad news about his brother-in-law. "Okay, Bethany, what's up? Is something wrong with Rob?"

"No," she hastened to assure him. "He's okay. It's not about him, it's about me." She blew out a long breath. "I want to stay here another three weeks."

This wasn't what Cody had expected to hear. He didn't have time to respond before his sister rushed into an explanation.

"Listen, Cody, I wouldn't ask if it wasn't important. And believe you me, I miss the boys so badly that I can't believe I'm saying this, but I need to stay here for a few more weeks. I'm making great progress but I'm not ready to come home. Can you help me out and keep the boys a tiny bit longer? Please?"

She had him at please. Neither Bethany nor her husband Rob had ever asked Cody for a thing, but he'd virtually lived on their couch before he bought his ranch. He owed them. Tucson could wait. "Absolutely, you take as long as you need." He glanced in the direction of the booth. Mitchell, now in possession of a blue crayon, was coloring a strand of his brother's hair. "Don't you worry about a thing," Cody assured his sister. "I've got the boys covered."

"That I'd love to see." He could hear the relief in her laughter. "But seriously, thank you so much, Cody. I wouldn't ask if I didn't really believe I needed to do this."

"Hey, I know how hard it is to do what you're doing."

Bethany laughed again. "Oh, right, Mr. Six Pack Abs, what exactly do you know about trying to lose a hundred pounds? You're all muscle."

He grinned. "Aw, shucks, and here I thought you were going to say I was all heart."

"Well, that too. But we need to talk about the rodeo."

Cody took a deep breath, counted to five, and exhaled before he responded. "Tucson's not a big deal."

"Yes, it is," she countered.

"No, it's not." Cody ran a hand through his hair. "Look, sis, you mean more to me than the circuit. I can head up to Durango next month after you're back. Colorado is just as good as Arizona. The kids come first."

"It means the world to me that you'd say that but you don't have to make a choice."

Cody motioned across the restaurant for Brian to sit down. He could have sworn that last time they'd eaten here he'd told the boys that the booth wasn't a trampoline, especially not with their boots on. He turned his attention back to his conversation with his sister. "What were you saying?"

"The boys are being awfully quiet. Is everything okay there?"

"Yeah, absolutely," he assured her. And it was true enough, if pouring the contents of the salt shakers into a root beer bottle could be considered acceptable behavior. "We're just three bachelors out for a bite to eat. But I should probably wrap this up soon."

"I'm sending someone out to the ranch to help you out."

"I don't need any help," Cody protested. A vision of the mountain of laundry waiting back at the house popped into his mind, followed by an image of the stack of dishes in the sink. "I'm keeping up."

"I know, and I'm not trying to cross a line into your business, but we both know your sponsorship deal is on the line. I couldn't live with myself if I was the cause of you losing it. Can you honestly tell me that the deal will come through if you don't win in Tucson?"

Cody scuffed at the linoleum floor with the toe of his boot. "What kind of help are we talking about?"

"You remember me telling you about Tessa, one of the women I've met here? Well, she and her new husband Liam introduced me to a co-worker of his named Fiona. She's willing to come out and give you a hand."

Cody closed his eyes. He didn't want to miss the rodeo but neither did he want to leave the kids with a babysitter he didn't know. "I don't know."

"What if I pull rank as your big sister and tell you that the decision is out of your hands?"

He quickly saw that this was a battle he wasn't going to win. Best to give in without a fight. A bucking bronco he could handle. His sister when she had her mind set on something, not so much. "They're your kids, so finally it's your call. I trust you." But even if he went along with her plan, it didn't mean he had to like it.

"I adore you," Bethany assured him. "So do the kids."

They wouldn't for long, Cody reckoned, not once he got back to the table and took away the spoons they were using as drumsticks. Lucky for him, the waitresses and other patrons seemed to think the boys were adorable. Still, he needed to get over to the table and get things under control. "So you'll set it up?"

"Absolutely. I'll text you when Fiona's on her way."

Fiona. Cody couldn't shake an uneasy feeling. A vision of a stone-faced, female prison warden popped into his mind. "What if the boys don't like her?"

Again, Bethany laughed. "Trust me, you're all going to like her. A lot. Consider her an extra pair of hands and just accept the help, okay?"

After a quick goodbye, Cody powered off his phone and slipped it into his back pocket. He slid into the booth and fixed a stern stare on his nephews. "Guys, settle down. And put those hot dogs back in the buns."

Mitchell grinned. "They're not hot dogs. They're our swords."

Cody shook his head. His sister might think all they needed was an extra pair of hands but nothing short of a fairy god-mother was going to work with these kids.

3

F iona and Liam landed in a whirl of gold glitter. As it began to settle around them, Fiona wiped the remaining sparkles off of her shirt sleeves and shook out her hair before looking around. Her eyes swept across flat stretch of grassy pastureland. A few lone trees stood in defiance of the barren landscape, but the overall effect left Fiona feeling like she'd landed on another planet. She snuck a glance at Liam. To her annoyance, he stood, hands in his pockets, calmly surveying their surrounding as if they'd just landed on the most interesting place on earth. This 'calm under any circumstances' attitude was so Liam. And so not her.

"Well, what do you think?" he asked.

"You don't want to know." Fiona flicked a gold sparkle off of her arm. "Please tell me that this is a pit stop."

He laughed. "Nope, it's your final destination."

She held up her hand. "Correction, London is my final destination. This is only temporary." When he didn't immediately respond, she resisted the urge to shake him. Instead, she blew out a long breath. If there was ever a time to exercise self-control, this was it. "So where exactly are we?"

Liam gazed around without answering.

"You do know where we are, right?"

He turned back to her and grinned. "I do. I was just admiring the place. If I wasn't on my honeymoon, I wouldn't mind hanging out here for awhile."

Which made exactly one of them.

"But," he continued. "It's not exactly the kind of place that I think Tessa might like."

This observation Fiona wasn't going to touch with ten foot pole. Liam's high maintenance witch of a new wife was not her concern right now. "Liam, where exactly are we?"

"Welcome to the Flat Iron Ranch."

She pivoted around slowly to make sure she hadn't missed something. She hadn't. "I don't see a ranch."

"That's because we're in the middle of two hundred prime acres of Texas grassland. The main house is over there."

Fiona pushed her sunglasses up onto the top of her head and squinted into the bright sunlight but still she didn't see anything. Exasperated, she turned to her boss. "Is this all some sort of ruse to drive me mad so I can't go to London?"

Liam's face broke into a wide smile. "No, based on the trust in each other we've built over the years, I promise that this is a short-term assignment." He reached out and slung an arm over her shoulder. "As you well know, our whole purpose of being a Fairy Godperson is based on our desire to help people out of a pinch. By pitching in here for a short time, you're being a massive help to more people than you realize." He squeezed her shoulders. "I'm grateful to you."

"Hmmm," was all she could manage to say while still staying sincere. "Let's do this then. I guess we head up to the house first?"

Liam shook his head. "Not we. You."

Fiona's eyes widened. "You jest."

"Nope. I'm going to leave you here."

"Don't you dare." Panic and frustration warred for top billing in Fiona's mind.

Liam reached out and laid a gentle hand on her arm. "Fiona, my dear, you've faced far greater challenges than this, with much aplomb and much success, I might add." He leaned in and brushed a gentle kiss across her cheek. "Just remember to have some fun."

Fiona watched as he reached for his key-chain that doubled as a magic wand. "Wait, don't go just yet." She took a deep breath and squared her shoulders. "Can't you at least give me a bit of gold sparkle? Just in case I run into something I can't handle?"

"There's nothing here you can't handle. I promise you." Liam's smile was kind.

"But-"

Liam took a step back from her. "No buts, Fiona. You've got this." He tapped his keychain and metallic sparkles began to swirl around his ankles. "Call me when you get to London."

And then he was gone.

CODY WAITED until the kids were finished slurping up the last of their root beer floats before he broached the subject of leaving them with a stranger. "Does your mom ever leave you guys with a babysitter?"

They exchanged a quick glance before Brian spoke. "We're not babies."

"I know, you're proper little cowpokes, but I just wondered who stayed with you back at home when your mom went out." He studied their faces for a signs of distress at the thought of being left, but they certainly didn't look worried. "When I was little, and Grandma had to go somewhere, she always left your mom in charge of me. So that's why I wondered who she left you with."

CAROLINE MICKELSON

"We go everywhere with her," Mitchell said.

"Everywhere," his little brother agreed.

And this might well account for his sister's exhaustion.

"Except this time," Brian said. "This time we're with you."

Cody nodded. Why was this so hard? More importantly, why wasn't his sister the one having this conversation with the boys? It wasn't like she was in prison and limited to one phone call a day, for crying out loud. She was at a health spa. "Well, that's the thing, there's been a slight change of plans."

"We're going somewhere?" Mitchell's eyes were wide.

He shook his head. "Nope. I am." He couldn't help but smile at their incredulous expressions. "Your mom asked a friend to come and stay with you while I'm gone."

"What friend?"

"Fiona."

"Never heard of her." Mitchell's response was emphatic and his expression dubious. He looked at his little brother. "You?"

Brian shook his head. "Are you sure

30

about this, Uncle Cody?"

And there was the crux of things. He wasn't sure at all that this was a good idea. Or the right thing to do, despite Bethany's assurance that it was. How was he supposed to hitch up and pull out with these two little buckaroos left behind with a woman he didn't know from Eve? "Well, I trust your mom to make the right choice by you two."

"Where are you going?" Mitchell demanded. "And why can't we come with you?"

"I've got to head out to Tucson for a rodeo. It's a big one and I need to be there."

The boys exchanged surreptitious glances. "We love Tucson," Mitchell said.

Brian's nod was enthusiastic. "Love it."

Cody took a sip of his coffee in an effort to hide his smile. "You guys have been there?"

Again with the nods, but this time they avoided looking at him. Exactly what he'd thought. "Guys, a rodeo isn't a place for two little boys to be unsupervised. I'll be too busy to keep an eye on you."

"We'll supervise each other," Mitchell

promised.

"And we won't try to ride any bulls," Brian offered as an attempt to sweeten the pot, not realizing that he'd just driven the final nail into the coffin. "Honest."

Cody forced himself to smile. "No can do, guys. We've got to do this your mom's way."

"What did you say the stranger's name was?" Mitchell asked.

"Fiona."

The boys each pulled a face that didn't bode well for his sister's choice of sitters.

"Hey, none of that now," Cody said, as he motioned for them to slide out of the booth. "Let's at least give her a chance."

He was talking to himself as much as he was to the boys.

FIONA PICKED her way through dirt, patches of mud, and assorted piles of proof that this was indeed a working cattle ranch, as she made her way up to the main ranch house. When she passed a pen of horses, they neighed loudly enough that she swore they were mocking the way she was tip-toeing through the dust. She stopped and stared at a brown horse. "Don't look at me like that. These espadrilles are less than a week old." She stared down at her shoes in dismay. They were so caked with mud that it was impossible to see that they'd recently been a lovely shade of green. "Now they're ruined."

The horse snorted, swished its tail from side to side, and then, clearly bored, walked away.

Fiona sighed, picked up her suitcase, squared her shoulders, and trudged toward the house. She had no doubt that the shoes were only the first of several sacrifices she'd need to make in the days ahead. But she could handle this, even without the use of her magic. And she could get new shoes once she was in London.

She'd just climbed the front porch and knocked on the front door when she heard the loud rumble of a diesel engine. Curious, she turned and watched as a huge pick-up truck bounced up the driveway, leaving a trail of dust in its wake. She'd never imagined that Texas would be so...well...dusty. She craned her neck to get a better view but the setting sun hit the windshield at an angle that made it impossible to clearly see the occupants of the truck.

She leaned against the porch railing and watched as the pick-up pulled to a stop in front of the house. A man slid out of the driver's side and slammed his door shut. His boots crunched over the gravel as he made his way toward her. In the time it took for him to reach her, she couldn't help but notice how perfectly his blue jeans fit him, how the white of crisp cotton shirt accentuated his suntanned skin, and that his belt buckle was as big as her fist. Realizing that she was holding her breath, she forced herself to exhale.

The cowboy stopped at the bottom of the three wooden steps and took off his hat. His eyes, the color of a blue summer sky, met and held hers for a full moment before he spoke. "Evening, Ma'am."

And with those words, Fiona realized one more thing.

She was in trouble.

4

Cody watched as the stranger standing on his front porch blinked rapidly several times in response to his greeting. He glanced backwards at the truck and was relieved to see his nephews sitting quietly just as he'd asked them to. He turned his attention back to the pretty brunette that stood between him and his front door. "Can I help you?"

She stared at him for another full minute before she nodded her head. "No." Reversing that answer, she then shook her head from side to side. "I mean, yes."

"Yes?" he prompted her when it appeared that was all she was going to say. "What's wrong? Are you lost?" Heaven knew she looked it.

"I don't think so." She looked over his shoulder in the direction of the truck and then back at him. "I'm Fiona Cantrell."

He took the hand she held out and shook it. "I thought as much." Although he'd not expected her to be this young. Or this pretty. For some reason, it unsettled him. He'd have much preferred it if she'd resembled the battle-axe he'd imagined her to be. "I'm Cody Proctor. But you already know that seeing as how you know my sister."

But when she opened her mouth to respond, her words were interrupted by a blaring honking sound coming from his truck. He flashed her an apologetic grin. "Let me just grab the boys," he shouted over the noise.

He jogged over to the truck and yanked open the passenger side door. "That's enough, right there," he warned Brian, whose right hand was poised to strike the steering wheel.

"But I didn't get my turn."

Cody reached in and swung Mitchell out

of the truck's cab and onto the gravel. He
then leveled as stern a look as he could
manage at Brian. "Next time. Right now we
need to get a move on."

This appeared to be an insufficiently
convincing explanation to Brian. "I wanna
honk it this time." But his interest was
quickly diverted as he leaned backward to
see past Cody. "Who's that pretty lady that
Mitchell's talking to?"

Cody whirled around and saw that
Mitchell was no longer standing right next
to him. He shook his head. His nephew
could be louder than a raging bull at times
and yet quieter than a cat at others. He held
out his hand to Brian. "Come meet her
yourself."

"Is she your girlfriend?"

"No, and that's enough questions. Let's
move." He stood back when Brian insisted
on jumping out of the truck by himself.
"Now mind your manners," he whispered as
they approached the porch.

But he needn't have worried because
Brian marched straight up the porch steps,
stuck his hand out for Fiona to shake and

introduced himself in a manner that would have done his mother proud.

Cody watched as Fiona knelt down so that she was at the boy's eye level. She'd lost her deer in the headlights look, and the smile she directed at his nephews was friendly. Perhaps his sister did know what she was doing by sending Fiona here.

"It's a pleasure to meet you, Mitchell," Fiona said. "I'm a friend of your mom's. I've come to spend a few days with you and your brother."

Mitchell nodded seriously. "I know. My uncle told us."

Fiona shot Cody a quick glance but he couldn't read her expression. "Did he, now?"

"He also said-"

Cody took that as his cue to move them all in indoors. "Boys, let's invite our guest in-side." He slipped past the boys and unlocked the front door. "Here, Mitchell, you hold the door for Miss Cantrell while I take her bag."

But this arrangement obviously didn't suit their guest. She snatched up her suit-case and he could swear her knuckles were practically white the way she was gripping it. He met her gaze.

"I've got it," she said. "And call me Fiona, please."

"Fiona, Fiona, Fiona," the boys sang in unison as they scampered into the house ahead of the adults.

"They're adorable boys."

"They're rascals, pure and simple." But as soon as the words were out of his mouth, he realized he wasn't helping their case. "Just full of energy. Regular little boys, you know." Heaven help him, he was officially babbling. "Come on in."

He watched as Fiona's gaze swept the room. He was glad for her curiosity because it gave him time to study her. She was nothing like he'd expected. For starters, she was younger than he'd thought she'd be. She was petite with a hourglass figure, certainly prettier than any other young woman he'd ever met. He cast around for a neutral, ice-breaking subject. "Your shoes are dirty. Looks like you came up through the back forty."

As soon as he saw her face flush, Cody realized he'd said the wrong thing. Again.

"I'm not sure what 'the back forty' means but I did cut across your land." She slipped off her shoes and hastily deposited them out on the front porch. "Sorry about that."

He shrugged, hoping to look nonchalant even thought he felt anything but. "No big deal, this is a working ranch." He motioned toward his boots. "We're always tracking dirt in."

"It looks fine," Fiona assured him. "I know I didn't give you much notice."

He motioned toward the sofa. "Why don't you have a seat here while I get your room ready?"

Once she was seated, he called out for his nephews to join them. They came busting out of their bedroom, nearly trampling each other to get to him. He grabbed one with each hand and pulled them close to him. "Okay, time to settle down, you two. Listen, I want you to impress Miss Fiona with your good manners. Why don't you bring her a cold drink while I see to her room?" He fixed a stern gaze on them in turn. "Can you do that for me?"

They nodded solemnly enough that he released his hold on them. He felt a surge of hope as they walked sedately toward the kitchen. They could do calm. Sometimes. He turned to his guest. "I'll be right back. Holler if you need me."

As quickly as he could, he grabbed a set of fresh sheets from the linen closet and stripped the bed in the guest room. That was the easy part though. Wrangling the fitted sheet onto the mattress proved more challenging than roping a calf. As he settled the top sheet onto the bed he congratulated himself on the silence coming from the living room. That could only mean that the boys had served their guest some lemonade and were now, hopefully, making polite conversation like two little gentleman. His lips stretched into a satisfied smile. Maybe there was a chance this could all work out long enough for him to get to Arizona, compete for a few days, and get back home before the kids even realized he was gone.

But then, in rapid succession, he heard a

scream, the sound of glass shattering, and finally the slamming of the front door. He tossed the pillow cases on the bed and ran down the hallway. "What's wrong? What happened?"

The boys were nowhere in sight. He watched as Fiona stood up from the couch, her hands covering her stomach. Cody sucked in his breath when he saw the seeping red stain that covered the front of her white dress. "What did they do to you?"

"IT'S FRUIT PUNCH," Fiona assured Cody. "It's fine. No harm done." She smiled and shrugged. "If you can show me which room I'll be staying in, I'll just change out of this."

"But what happened?"

Wasn't it self-explanatory? She looked down at the round red stain on her dress. She looked like she was wearing a Japanese flag.

"Are you hurt?"

Fiona shook her head, too many questions swirled around her mind for her to form a coherent answer. Why on earth did he look so panicked? This was a man who rode bucking broncos? And most pressing of all, where had the boys torn off to? She forced herself to speak. "It was a simple mistake. So please just show me where to change and then maybe you can go look for the boys?"

Cody took her suitcase and motioned for her to follow him down the hall. He stopped in front of an open door. "I didn't finish making the bed."

Fiona stepped inside the bedroom. A white iron single bed stood against the far wall under the window. White eyelet curtains fluttered in the delicate breeze coming in through the window. A white and lavender wedding ring quilt hung on one wall, and a matching one covered the bed. A tall white wooden bookcase stood against the opposite wall. The overall effect was absolutely charming. "It's lovely."

"It was my sister's room when we were growing up." He deposited her suitcase on the round braided rug. "I'll leave you to change while I go rustle up the kids." He paused in the doorway, his expression apologetic. "I'm sorry," he said, "about your dress and everything."

Fiona waved her hand to dismiss his concern, startled by just how odd it felt not to have a wand in her hand. A little magic right now would certainly save her dress and shoes from absolute ruin. But she had just enough glitter to get to London and she wasn't about to waste it trying to save an outfit, no matter how cute it was. Besides, if the rest of her stay at the Flat Iron Ranch was anything at all like this first forty-five minutes had been, she was going to have to learn how to fend for herself without the benefit of magic. She turned her attention back to Cody. "It's just a dress. Let's let it go. I'm more interested in where the boys went. Do you think they're in danger?"

Cody's smile was swift. "No, but I can't say the same for whomever they're pestering at the moment."

"Then give me a second to change and I'll come with you to find them. If that's okay."

He nodded. "I'll meet you out front." His

eyes swept the length of her and settled on her trashed espadrilles. "I'll dig up a pair of boots for you if you tell me what size you wear."

Once he was duly dispatched to look for a size seven boot, Fiona quickly changed into what she thought was appropriate ranch wear. Not that she'd really known what to pack, having never been any closer to a working cattle ranch than she had to the moon. But she did have several pair of jeans with crystal encrusted back pockets. To accompany her designer denim, she chose a red shantung silk sleeveless top and, after a brief hesitation, she grabbed a cropped white leather jacket before she wadded up her dress and shoes and tossed them into the corner. She had her work cut out for her over the next several days. Stain removal wasn't a top priority.

Just as he'd promised, Cody was waiting on the front porch with a pair of black leather cowboy boots. Fiona reached out for them. "These look practically new."

"They're Bethany's but she rarely gets out here anymore."

Fiona turned them back and forth, carefully inspecting their workmanship. "You know, if they'd used red accent stitching instead of white, I think these would be adorable."

Cody's expression was puzzled. "What are you talking about?"

"Never mind." She slipped them on, carefully tucking her jeans into the boots, pleased that the fit was close to perfect. She smiled at him. "So where do you think we'll find your nephews?"

Cody ran a hand through his hair and put his cowboy hat back on. "Right smack in the middle of trouble, I don't doubt."

Fiona laughed. Bethany's cowboy brother was far more handsome than she'd expected, not to mention disarmingly charming. She'd have to watch her step at the ranch, figuratively as well as literally.

They cut across the front yard and followed the sound of barking dogs that was coming from behind the front barn. The dogs were barking, baying, and howling, all at the same time, in decibel defying unison. "How many dogs do you have?"

He shook his head ruefully. "Not as many as you'd imagine judging by all that racket." He took off at a jog. "Sounds like they need rescuing," he called over his shoulder.

She assumed by 'they', he meant the dogs and not his nephews.

She rounded the corner of the barn just in time to see Cody lunge for the younger of the two boys. Lunge and miss, thanks to a Shepherd mix that was hell bent on escaping from the impromptu doggie wash that the boys had set up. The dog barreled into Cody, knocking him sideways. Fiona opened her mouth to warn Cody about the buckets of sudsy water he was about to topple over, except that her words of caution were drowned out when the boys turned the hose on her. Her words ended up coming out as unintelligible spluttering sounds as she held up her hands to block the water that was spraying all over her.

"Boys, enough," Cody yelled loudly enough that his voice drowned out the dogs. "Stop, NOW."

'Now' must have been the magic word

because the soaking immediately stopped. Fiona shook her head from side to side and then wiped the water that dripped down her face. She didn't even bother to look down at her clothing. The leather she could probably save but her top was beyond repair. Shantung silk and water mixed together about as well as vinegar and oil.

"What in blue blazes are you two up to?" Cody demanded. "No, wait, don't tell me." He turned to Fiona. "Are you okay?"

If okay meant alive, then yes she was. And if his question also meant 'are you aware that you're completely in over your head here?', then, the answer to that was also a yes. "I'm fine."

"We're sorry, Uncle Cody," Brian said. "Honest we are."

Mitchell nodded enthusiastically. Obviously he thought it wiser to keep quiet. Smart boy.

Fiona watched as Cody took off his hat and shook the water off of it. Although she'd known him only about an hour, she didn't think he looked angry. More like exasperated. She experienced a sudden surge of sympathy for him. Although she couldn't do anything in her official capacity as a Fairy Godmother, she could still be of some help.

She clapped her hands together loudly enough that the little boys turned to look at her. "Okay, guys," she said, "here's what we're going to do. I want you to turn off one hose and carefully hand me the other one. I'm going to rinse the dogs off one at a time while you empty the buckets and wring out the sponges. We're going to work quickly and quietly, is that clear?"

They nodded in unison.

"Good, then let's go." She reached out for a hose and motioned for Mitchell to lead one of the dogs over. "Stand there and hold his collar while I rinse him off, please."

She turned her attention to a black Labrador and made short work of rinsing him off. "Next, please."

So intent was she on her work that she jumped when Cody's hand closed over hers.

"Here, let me," he said, his voice apologetic. "You've gone above and beyond."

She glanced over her shoulder at Brian

and was relieved to see that he was quietly focused on rinsing the soap out of the buckets. "Something tells me that this is business as usual around here?"

He nodded sheepishly. "Can you tell I don't have a lot of experience with kids? I must be doing something very wrong. Why don't you go on up to the house and get changed." He gave her a half grin. "Again. And if you wouldn't mind making it, I'd love if you'd join me for a hot cup of coffee when I get up there."

She nodded. "If you're sure you've got everything under control?"

He laughed. "I'd be a liar if I said that. But I think I can get this all cleaned up without incident."

"Coffee it is, then. See you up the house."

But she hadn't taken more than fifteen steps before Cody called out to her. She whirled around.

"Look, Fiona, I know this is way more than Bethany meant for you to handle. You don't have to stay and deal with this."

Oh, but she did. Because Fiona knew without a shadow of a doubt that this little favor Liam had asked of her wasn't a favor at all. Or an assignment. It was a test. A test of her nerves, of her resolve to do whatever she had to do to get to London, and a test of her strength in resisting the charm of a certain handsome cowboy.

And it was a test she was going to ace.

5

When Fiona staggered out to the kitchen the next morning, her only real goal was to find some form of caffeine. Preferably liquid, but after the night she'd spent tossing and turning, she wasn't in a position to be picky. She'd thrown on a black tank top with a black blouse over it, knotted at the waist, and a pair of white jeans. She knew full well that her jeans were unlikely to stay white past noon if Bethany's sons had anything to say about it. Still, she had fashion standards to uphold.

She found the kitchen empty. The smell of coffee lingered in the air and she inhaled deeply as she filled a mug. One sip assured

her that she'd make it through the morning.
It was black and strong, just how she liked
it. Only after a few more appreciative sips
did she notice a folded sheet of paper with
her name on it propped up against the sugar
bowl. She reached out for it.

*Morning - I've got the boys with me. See you
at lunch. - Cody*

Fiona smiled. So Cody Proctor was a
man of few words, somehow that didn't
surprise her. She pulled out a chair and sank
into it, her hands cradling the warm coffee
cup. To say she'd been impressed with
Bethany's brother was an understatement.
Truthfully, she hadn't put much thought
into what he was going to be like before she
arrived. She'd been far more wrapped up in
her own agenda, namely getting this assignment over so she could get to London. A
quick glance at the clock over the stove told
her that she had a few hours before
lunchtime. She took a last sip of coffee,
rinsed it out, and left it on the sink's drain
board. Time to get to work.

And work there was to do. In spades.
After a cursory examination of the house,

Fiona felt as exhausted as if she'd just built the place from the ground up. Piles of clothes overflowed from baskets that filled up every square inch of the laundry room. The way the clothing was haphazardly thrown in the baskets left her with little hope that it had been washed, fluffed and folded already.

The bathrooms, she was relieved to discover, were clean. She couldn't say the same for the boys' room. It was a few dirty socks short of being declared a natural disaster. She leaned against the doorway and surveyed the mess. It was probably a safe assumption that the two large mounds in the center of the room were twin beds buried under toys, stuffed animals, yet more clothes, and heaven knew what else. She frowned. Yesterday, when she'd first met Cody and the boys, they'd all been dressed in clean clothes. The kitchen and bathrooms were fairly tidy. So it appeared that some cleaning got done, just no laundry or straightening up. What was that about?

Deciding that only fifty or sixty wash and dry cycles stood between her and tidiness, Fiona tackled the laundry first. She'd just tossed a load of towels into the dryer when her cell phone notified her that she had a text message. She pulled the phone out of her back pocket, assuming it was Liam checking up on her.

It wasn't Liam. It was Tessa.

Tessa: Meanwhile, back at the ranch...

Fiona rolled her eyes. She didn't have time for this.

Fiona: Your question?

Tessa: How long until you cry uncle and Liam has to swoop in to save the day?

Fiona: Not going to happen. Everything's fine here. Better than fine.

Tessa: Right! I bet you're dying to whip out a magic wand and let glitter get you out of the mess you're in.

True, but Fiona would rather kiss a frog than admit it. Especially to Liam's wife.

Fiona: Wrong again. Now, if you don't want anything, I'm going to get back to sunbathing and my Margarita.

Tessa: Just tell me how handsome your cowboy is...I'd hate to be the only one who is enjoying the attention of a gorgeous man.

Fiona: Speaking of which, why don't you go bother your poor husband?

Tessa: He's busy planning our extended honeymoon. Hopefully we'll be going someplace exciting. London, perhaps?

Fiona: Goodbye, Tessa. BTW, you're such a witch!

Tessa: I know. Don't be jealous.

Exasperated, Fiona clicked her phone off and shoved it back into her pocket. Work was what she needed to distract herself. Separating whites and darks into piles kept her hands busy. *Don't be jealous.* Ugh. That comment was classic Tessa. What Liam saw in Tessa was beyond Fiona's comprehension but he seemed happy with the queen of snark. That was all that mattered.

And hadn't it all worked out for the best? Once both in the running for the job with the European Paranormal Council, Liam and Tessa had fallen in love and decided that neither of them would take the job. Which was how Fiona had ended up being nominated. It didn't bother her in the slightest that she had the job by default. Once she was in office, she'd work triple

time to impress the council. All she had to
do was get to London.

She slammed the clothes washer lid and
buried her face in her hands. '*London, perhaps?*' replayed in her mind. Was it just Tessa
being Tessa or were her words a thinly
veiled hint that she didn't have the job as
sewn up as she thought?

Enough. She had to get a grip. There was
a reason why she was here at the Flat Iron
Ranch. What exactly that reason was, Fiona
couldn't begin to fathom but that didn't
mean that there wasn't one. Sitting around
torturing herself with questions no one
could answer wasn't how she was going to
pass whatever kind of test this was, nor was
it the best way to stay sane.

She grabbed a bucket and a mop and
tackled the kitchen floor. Figuring out how
to use the vacuum was a bit more tricky. At
home she used gold glitter to keep her home
spotless. But that was there, where she had
access to glitter galore. Here she had a precious little amount, certainly not enough to
consider wasting even one tiny sparkle on
housework. Or laundry. Or cooking.

As she worked, Fiona studied her surroundings in a bid to learn more about Bethany's brother. Not that she'd snoop. Ever. But even if she'd been willing to, there was precious little about to look through. Cody probably spent most of his time out in the pasture. Or field. Or whatever they called acreage in Texas. She straightened a stack of publications from someplace called PRCA which, upon a closer look, stood for Professional Rodeo Cowboys Association. Professional cowboys? The thought made her smile. Who knew?

A quick glance at her watch reminded Fiona that she was going to have to hurry if she wanted things tidied up before Cody and the boys headed in for lunch. Overall she was satisfied with her efforts, the only thing she was behind on was the laundry but that would take either three days or a miracle to catch up on.

The back door slammed open. "Miss Fiona? Where are you?"

She tossed aside the towel she was folding and hustled out to where the boys were. "What's wrong?"

"It's bad." Mitchell bent over double as he struggled to catch his breath.

Fiona's eyes widened. She turned her attention to his brother. "Tell me what's wrong, Brian." Her breath caught in her throat. Oh, God, was it Cody? Had something happened to him? "Is something wrong with your uncle?"

Brian nodded. "Yes, ma'am."

But something in the way his eyes sparkled warned Fiona they were having her on. She blew out a deep breath, willing her heart to stop racing. "What's wrong with him?"

"He's hungry." Mitchell burst into a fit of giggles.

Fiona rolled her eyes. "Funny, you both got me. Now, is he the only one who's hungry? Because if you're not, then I'd suggest you head into your room and start straightening up."

This sobered the two little cowboys up quickly.

"I'm near starvation," Brian said. "Mitchell too."

"You'll need to wash up, both of you." She

ignored their frowns. "Go do that and then come show me your sparkling clean hands."

Brian furrowed his brow. "Boys don't have sparkling hands."

She couldn't help but smile. "Fine. Go wash and then come show me your regular old clean hands, okay?"

Once she heard the water running, Fiona took a quick inventory of the refrigerator. The contents weren't exactly sparse but it was evident that Cody didn't harbor dreams of becoming a master chef if the cowboy thing didn't work out. Not that her culinary skills were anything to brag about. Take-out was her personal specialty.

She pulled out a package of hot dogs. Hadn't she seen a barbeque grill on the back deck? She was sure she had. But she was also sure that she didn't want to light the grill and then watch as Bethany's boys found a way to burn down the house. She put the hot dogs back and pulled out a package of bacon and a carton of eggs instead.

As the bacon sizzled in the frying pan, Fiona whipped a dozen eggs into the same frenzied state that her mind was in. She knew the fate of the eggs, her own she wasn't so sure about. What was she *really* doing here?

Two tornados disguised as little boys tore through the kitchen. Fiona jumped between a curious Brian and the stove, clutching a wooden spoon as her only line of defense. "Be careful. The stove is hot."

"We want to help."

Exactly what she was afraid of. "That's great. But do you know what would really help me? If you would set the table."

"Boring."

Fiona did her best to raise one eyebrow the way her mother had done years ago. Judging by Mitchell's unimpressed expression, she had some practicing to do. "It's not boring to me. I still don't know where everything is."

Mitchell shrugged. "Okay, I'll do it."

"I'll take care of the bacon," Brian said from behind her.

Fiona whirled around to see that the five-year-old had managed to get behind her and he had one hand on the frying pan's handle. He held a fork in the other hand. He was still short enough that he had to reach up to get a good grip on the pan, which meant that with one false move he was apt to bring the hot contents down.

"That's so helpful of you." She kept her voice low and calm as if she was talking him off a ledge. She took a step closer, anxious not to startle him. "May I please have a look?"

Brian stood back just enough so that she could lean over the stove but he kept his grip firmly on the frying pan.

"Can I show you how I flip the bacon with a fork?" Fiona asked. To her immense relief, he nodded and relinquished his hold on the pan.

Fiona sagged with relief once she regained control of the hot stovetop. She'd never given much thought to the intricacies of child care but she was rapidly beginning to believe that mothers of young child should be given combat pay in addition to three paid weeks of vacation a year. She glanced up and through the window over the sink. Cody was walking toward the house. A ripple of excitement ran through her at the sight of him.

"It's my turn, let go."

Brian's muffled answer meant a tussle was afoot.

Fiona moved the bacon onto the back burner and turned around to diffuse the disagreement. "Boys, what are you-" but a half gallon of orange juice, without the lid on, flew out of the boys' hands and doused her in sticky citrus juice, effectively answering her question.

"Uh, oh," Mitchell said. "We didn't mean for that to happen."

Fiona wiped a few droplets from her face. The front of her shirt was drenched. She closed her eyes. This was a test. Not one she understood, but one she wanted to pass. She opened her eyes. "I know you didn't. But we've got to get this cleaned up." She quickly unbuttoned her blouse and slipped it off, fortunately her tank top was still dry. "I want you both to go into the laundry room and get some rags. I'm going to change my shirt and then we'll take care of this."

She turned back to the stove, turned off the burners, and then washed her hands in the sink. When she turned back around she was surprised to see the boys hadn't moved. They were rooted in place, their eyes wide.

Cody stood in the doorway. His expression mirrored the shock on his nephews' faces.

"Cody, what's wrong?"

His eyes didn't leave hers. He took off his hat and held it over his chest. "It's your...um...we saw your, uh-"

But Mitchell didn't wait for his uncle to find the right words. "Miss Fiona, why do you have wings?"

6

Cody swung his pick-up into the only empty spot in the parking lot and cut the engine. He wasn't sure if taking Fiona out to dinner was apology enough for how uncomfortable he and the boys had made her feel about her tattoo but he hoped it would be a start. He was no expert on women but he could have sworn that he saw sheer panic flash through her eyes when Mitchell had asked if she had wings. Though why she'd have a fearful reaction, he couldn't fathom. It couldn't possibly come as a surprise to her that the intricate design of her tattoo looked like wings.

He unfastened his seat belt and turned to

face her. "Ready for some of the best bar-beque east of the Rio Grande?"

Fiona peered up at the glowing red neon sign. "The Deep Pit," she read aloud before turning to look at him. "Quite the name, isn't it?"

Her smile set his heart to racing. He couldn't help but smile in return. Fiona Cantrell was like no woman he'd ever met before. Cody was shy, normally more confident around horses than ladies, but there was something about Fiona that made him feel at ease. Which should make him uneasy, he reasoned, but somehow it didn't. "Twenty bucks says that in two hours you'll tell me it's the best barbeque you've ever tasted."

"No deal." She popped open her door and slid out of the truck. "That's a sucker's bet considering that I've never eaten bar-beque before."

He hopped down from the driver's seat and reached into the backseat to help his nephews out. "How's that even possible?" he asked her. "Unless you've been living in a penthouse somewhere where they only

serve fancy finger food?" As he spoke he realized that he had no idea what part of the
country she originally hailed from. "Where's
home, anyway?"

"Here and there. It's a long story." She
flashed him another shy smile and reached
out for Brian's hand. "I'm not the only one
who's hungry, am I?"

The Deep Pit was at its usual near capacity crowd but they didn't have to wait
more than ten minutes for a table. The at-
mosphere was sawdust-on-the-floor casual. Honky tonk music played in the
background, accompanied by the familiar
chaotic sounds of a family restaurant.
Cody held a chair out for Fiona, waited
while the boys sat on either side of her,
and then he took the seat opposite her. Before they'd left the house, he'd secured a
promise from both boys that they would
issue Fiona a world class apology. And it
was a promise he intended for them to
keep.

"Isn't there something you two want to
say to our guest?" he prompted them.

Brian slid down a few inches in his chair

and shot his older brother a worried look. Mitchell, however, appeared undaunted.

"Miss Fiona, wouldn't you like an ice cold beer?"

Before Cody could recover from his surprise and think of how to respond to such an outrageous detour from the agreed upon script, Fiona clapped her hands together and laughed.

"Oh, Mitchell, I just never know what you're going to say or do next."

Cody shook his head. "I guess that's a part of his charm."

"A big part," she agreed. "Now, to answer your question, I've actually never had a beer but I'm up for trying it."

The arrival of their waitress gave Cody an opportunity to hide his surprise at her admission. He didn't think he'd ever met anyone who hadn't ever drank a beer before, but while this had caught him off guard perhaps it shouldn't have. Fiona was unlike the women he was used to. She was beautiful without being overtly glamorous, polished without being even a bit pretentious, and somehow she came across as both gentle and strong. A woman in a million.

After he placed an order for two long-necks and two glasses of lemonade, he forced himself to focus on what really needed to happen. "Mitchell, Brian, isn't there something you'd like to say to Miss Fiona?" he prompted them again.

"We're sorry about ruining your dress," Brian kicked off the litany of their misdeeds that required apologies. "I tripped on the rug."

"And I'm sorry I turned the hose on you," his brother added. "But we thought we were doing a good thing by giving the dogs a bath."

"Oh, don't forget the orange juice." Brian was clearly warming to the topic. "We got your shirt all wet and the floor was really sticky, wasn't it?" He sounded more proud of that than contrite.

"I appreciate your apologies," Fiona told them. "I know your intentions were good. I happen to believe that's what matters most."

Mitchell leaned forward, his face earnest. "We're also sorry for asking about your wings. Uncle Cody told us that was none of our business." He shot a glance at Cody, who nodded in agreement.

"It almost looks like you could fly," Brian threw in.

"Boys, enough, what did we talk about at home?" Cody chided them. Honestly, no one could hold a candle to these two in the impertinence department. "Your mom sent Fiona here to help us out, not to be grilled. Got it?" Once they both nodded, he turned his attention to Fiona. "I'm sorry."

"It's okay," she said.

Still, it didn't escape his notice that she drew her sweater a bit closer around her. He could certainly understand her reluctance to have her tattoo discussed so brazenly when they'd all only just met. But he could also understand his nephews' fascination. He'd never seen anything in all of his life as amazing as the delicately etched design that looked like it covered her entire back. Perhaps it had been the light playing a trick, but it was almost as if the wings were made of gold. The boys swore they thought her tattoo actually glimmered, and a part of him agreed even though it couldn't be possible.

He took a long sip of beer and forced himself to look away from Fiona. He was a confirmed bachelor, more committed to the rodeo circuit than to the idea of settling down. His attraction to any woman, even one as flat out amazing as Fiona, was a distraction he couldn't afford. It was a good thing he was pulling out for Tucson in a couple of days.

Their meal was over way too quickly. He and the boys enjoyed watching Fiona try to delicately eat her ribs with a knife and fork. They'd given her a round of applause when she finally gave up and set her utensils aside. She was an absolute natural with the kids, not to mention pleasant and engaging when several friends had come over to say hello. As Cody settled the bill, he realized that he'd enjoyed the evening far more than any other.

Neither could he remember ever having met anyone who managed to bob, weave, and duck questions about herself like Fiona managed to. Despite his efforts, he'd learned exactly nothing about her. Just how much did his sister actually know about Fiona? He decided to give her a call right after he got the boys to bed.

But that particular task proved to be nearly impossible. The boys refused to stay in bed. Trying to get them down for the night had been like one of those annoying county fair games where you'd whack one mole and another would pop up.

"They behaved beautifully at the restaurant." Fiona plopped down next to him on the front porch steps, her second-ever bottle of beer in hand. "Maybe they just need to get their pent-up energy out?"

"A very diplomatic explanation for the insanity that has occurred within the last hour and a half." Cody leaned back on his elbows and turned to look at her. "Do you have a background in diplomacy by any chance?"

She laughed. "Sorry, no, but I've worked with a fair share of my clients who needed careful handling, I guess you could say. But kids are pretty new to me."

"Me too. As you can see, they're kicking my backside."

"Don't be so hard on yourself. I think you're doing great."

"Thanks." He felt oddly pleased by her praise. And also equally concerned. "Look, I know my sister asked you to come take care of the boys, and I think it's great that you were willing. But they're a handful, at the best of times." He watched as she took a sip of from her beer bottle. Her hands were delicate, and her neck was long and graceful. He forced himself to look away. "I'm worried about leaving you alone here with them."

"I thought you said that your ranch manager and his wife were going to be here the whole time."

He nodded. "Well, yeah, they will be. And in an emergency they'll do whatever they can to help you out but I'm more concerned about the day to day craziness."

"It's quiet now."

It was at that. The boys must have finally fallen asleep. Perhaps being chased back to bed fourteen times had exhausted them. It had him.

"I can do this, Cody. I know it's scary for you to leave Mitchell and Brian with someone you don't know well but I'll guard them with my life."

He sat up and turned to face her. He didn't want to leave her in a situation where she was in over her head. Heck, he didn't want to leave her, period. "That's not what I'm worried about."

"So what exactly is the problem?"

His shrug was far more casual than his inner turmoil felt. "I guess I want to be in two places at once."

"It's that important that you go?"

He nodded. "The chance to score the prize money isn't something I can afford to pass up. And if I win, it'll seal a very lucrative promotional deal."

"Then you should go."

"Yeah, but rodeo is a sport that requires intense concentration." His gaze held hers. "I can't compete if I'm worried about leaving you behind here."

"I get how important this is to you.

Bethany knew that too if she went to all the trouble to arrange for me to be here." She reached over and gently touched his arm. "You should go, Cody. We'll wait here for you."

Fiona's words radiated empathy, and her voice was warm and encouraging. Sitting that close to her, with her attention solely focused on him, felt like she was casting a spell on him. Which, Cody later decided, was the reason he opened his mouth and said the last thing he expected to hear himself say.

"Come with me, Fiona. You and the boys." He took a deep breath for courage. "We'll all go to Tucson together."

A huge smile spread across her face. "You're sure?"

He nodded, although the only thing he was sure of at that exact moment in time was that her smile was a beautiful sight.

"Do you think the boys would enjoy going?"

"Would they ever, are you kidding?" He reached over and tucked a stray strand of hair behind her ear. He felt her shiver as his hand gently brushed her cheek. "Will you come?"

She hesitated for only a moment. "I'd love to."

He grinned. "Perfect."

But that night, as he lay in bed staring at the ceiling, he decided that the idea wasn't perfect. It was perfectly stupid. How on earth was he going to focus on competing if he couldn't take his mind off of Fiona? This wasn't his first rodeo. He knew exactly what happened to anyone who tried to go eight seconds if they weren't two thousand per-cent focused on their ride.

He rolled over and punched his pillow. As much as it galled him, first thing in the morning he was going to have to tell Fiona that he'd changed his mind. Spending near on a week in such close proximity to her was impossible. There was no way it would work.

7

"**O**f course, it will work." Fiona put her hands on her hips and stared at the pile of luggage waiting to be packed into the back of the truck. "Let me try."

Cody jumped down from the truck's bed. "Fine, if you've got a magic wand, then wave it."

Fiona resisted the urge to roll her eyes. As if he knew anything about magic wands. But they were running late and the last thing she felt like doing was arguing with him. Correction, the last thing she felt like doing was leaving some of her luggage in Texas when she needed it in Arizona. She'd nearly lost her mind trying to keep Mitchell and Brian under control when she'd taken them into town to shop with her. Who knew that spinning racks of clothing and dashing around the store while managing to touch every single item for sale was something little boys liked to do? Certainly, not her. But she'd managed to keep them from being arrested and locked up in juvenile detention, and she'd put together a new wardrobe worthy of a rodeo queen. She certainly wasn't about to concede defeat now.

"Fiona, we've got to leave in the next twenty minutes or we're going to get behind schedule." Cody stared down at her three suitcases. "Just pick one of them, for crying out loud."

"Are you two having a fight?" Brian asked.

"No." Fiona and Cody spoke in perfect unison.

"Sure looks like it from here," Mitchell called from the front porch steps. He leaned over and whispered something into his brother's ear. Whatever it was set Brian off in a fit of giggles.

Fiona turned back to Cody. She could

only deal with one male at a time. "I'm taking all three cases so if you really want to get on the road, I'd suggest that you find a way to squeeze them in with all of your paraphernalia."

"Paraphernalia?" He took off his hat and ran his hand through his hair.

She wished he wouldn't do that, he was beyond adorable when he did. He appeared oblivious to his own charm. At least she hoped he was unaware of how he affected her. Heaven knew she was doing everything she could to hide how attracted to him she was. "Paraphernalia means stuff. Belongings."

"I know what it means." He tossed his hat through the truck's open window. "But you can't really need all of this." His eyes met hers, his expression hopeful. "Can we compromise at two?"

Fiona shook her head. She was standing her ground on this one. "I think you're the one who's over-packed." She gestured to one of his boxes that he'd nestled in amongst the others as if it contained England's crown jewels. "Look how much room that thing takes up."

He took a step closer to her, close enough now that she had to tilt back her head or she'd be staring at his chest. Which wasn't entirely a bad thing, but she needed to keep her wits about her if she was going to get her way.

"That **thing** is my saddle."

"But you told me your event was bare-back bronc riding, right? So it would seem to me that your saddle isn't strictly necessary on this trip." She cocked her head to the side. "I've got you there, don't I, cowboy?"

CODY SETTLED his hands on his hips. "The only thing you've got is five minutes to fit your 'paraphernalia' into the truck, or we're pulling out without any of it."

His eyes held hers for a long moment, long enough for her to feel mesmerized.

"Can't you two kiss and make up?" Mitchell called from the steps. His words caused his little brother to laugh so hard that he doubled over, clutching at his stomach.

Fiona held her breath as Cody dropped his gaze to her lips. The boys laughter faded away as the sound of her heartbeat grew louder in her own ears. The idea that Cody would kiss her was insanity, pure and simple. Certainly not what Bethany asked her to come here for. Not to mention Liam...but the very thought of her former boss was like a bucket of freezing cold water dumped over her head. Liam. Of course. This was her test. To see if she could resist temptation. And she had come dangerously close to failing. She stepped back just far enough that the moment was broken.

She turned to the boys. "You both run in use the bathroom again because we're ready to go." Once they did, she turned to Cody. "Don't you need to get your horse?"

"I'm not loading her up until I'm sure we're rolling out in less than five minutes."

Fiona waved her hand as if to dismiss him. "We are. You get the horse and I'll take care of the bags."

Cody blew out a breath that sounded

awfully exasperated to her ears. Well, he wasn't the only one nearing the end of his rope. But to his credit he didn't question her again, instead he turned and headed in the direction of the barn.

Once he was out of sight, Fiona looked over her shoulder to make sure the boys were still inside and that no ranch hands were looking. Satisfied that she was alone for a precious second, she took her key-chain sized wand and, without giving herself a split second to question her wisdom, or lack of, she flicked her wrist just enough that her luggage rose and settled itself neatly and securely in the truck bed. She bit her lip as she held the wand up in front of her. The tiny handle was made of Lucite, which gave her a clear view of how much gold glitter was left. Luckily she hadn't used too much. She slipped the wand back into her pocket

"But that's it," she said aloud. "Once and done. The rest is for London."

"Who's London?"

Fiona jumped at the sound of Mitchell's voice. "Where did you come from?"

"The bathroom." He looked from the ground to the back of the truck and back. "Did Uncle Cody pack your bags?"

She crossed her fingers behind her back. "I took care of them." Lying to children was so not cool. Time for a change of subject. "Where's Brian?"

Mitchell shrugged. "I dunno."

"Well, go find him please, and tell him we're ready to go."

It took him only a few minutes to rustle up his younger brother. By the time they were buckled in the truck, Cody had finished loading his horse into the trailer. And then, with a quick word to his ranch foreman, he swung himself up into the driver's seat. He fastened his seatbelt, fired up the truck, and turned to her. "Last chance to change your mind and stay here."

Fiona refused to consider that she was making a big mistake by going. Reason might dictate that she should stay at the house with the boys, it was definitely the safer choice. But safe wasn't what she wanted. Time with Cody was. "Let's roll."

To Cody's surprise, his nephews did their
level best to adhere to his rule that they
each could ask 'Are we there yet?' only once
per hour. He'd done his level best to explain
to them that they were staying overnight at
a friend's house in Las Cruces but they
seemed far more content when he just
threw a random number at them.

He glanced over at Fiona. Unfortunately,
content wasn't a word he could use to describe her. Not judging by the way she kept
shifting in her seat, at any rate. "What's
wrong?" he finally asked.

She turned to him, startled. "Nothing's
wrong. Why?"

"You seem fidgety." He turned his attention back to the road. "You don't get car
sick, do you?"

"I don't think so."

"You don't think so?" He shook his head.
"Seems like that's something you'd know."

But Fiona didn't respond, she just
shrugged and looked out the window.

And then it struck him that he'd made

precious little progress getting to know
anything about this woman. He knew almost nothing about her, well pretty darn
near close to nothing anyway. But he knew
how he felt about her, although he'd be
darned if he understood how he'd fallen so
far, so fast. But he wanted to know more
about her. And he knew just who to call in
for help. He glanced in the rear view mirror.
His nephews were awake, but quiet. Perfect.
"You guys up for a game of twenty
questions?"

He grinned as they both called 'Not it,' at
the same time. "Not it," he added. "That
leaves you in the hot seat, Fiona."

She twisted around in her seat as far as
her seatbelt would let her. Out of the
corner of his eye, he watched her smile at
the boys. "I've never played but I'll give it
a go."

And so the boys began their barrage.
Cody had to admire their stamina. They
volleyed question after question at her, the
huge majority of which were completely appropriate questions he was glad to note. Although a few were borderline nosey.

"Who was your first boyfriend?" Mitchell asked.

"That's easy. Douglas M. Pearson. Fourth grade."

Brian wasn't about to be outdone. "Who's your boyfriend now?"

"I don't have one," Fiona said.

"Why not?" Mitchell asked before Brian could ask the obvious follow-up question.

"I'm not sure," Fiona hedged. "I guess I've been really busy with my work. I travel a lot."

Neither of the boys had anything to follow that up with and Cody sensed they were rapidly losing interest but he felt like maybe, just maybe, he might be getting a bit closer to finding out just who Fiona Cantrell was. "Best road trip ever?"

"I'm going to have to say this one," she said after a brief pause. "Fair disclosure, it's my first road trip."

Cody hardly knew what to say to that. Starting at a very early age, he'd logged thousands of miles traveling to rodeos with his dad. "Best vacation ever?"

"A trip to the beach with my parents when I was six," she said.

"Don't tell me that was the only vacation you've ever had?"

She nodded. "It was hard for my parents to get away from work."

"What kind of work did they do?"

She hesitated for so long that he was certain she wasn't going to answer but she finally did.

"I guess you could say we all worked in the family business. Sort of a cross between event planning and providing the ultimate in customer care."

While that only made marginal sense to him, Cody didn't push her for an explanation. It was clear that she'd put an effort into answering it at all. "Last question, I promise," he said, feeling the need to push the envelope just that little bit further. "Tell me something that you're afraid of."

She didn't skip a beat. "I'm afraid of horses. You?"

Cody grinned. "Not me, I like to ride."

"That's not what I meant and you know it." She reached over and playfully punched his shoulder. "Play fair, Cody. What scares you?"

He glanced over and shook his head. "Cowboys aren't scared of anything, don't you know that?"

"You're not going to tell me?"

He thought a moment. There was no way he was going to confess that the idea of falling in love with Fiona, and then watching her walk away with his heart, was the scariest thing he could think of.

8

By the time Cody took the exit toward Las Cruces, the boys were fast asleep in the back seat and Fiona looked about ready to nod off herself. Although it was only a bit after six o'clock, the February night sky was dark. The only light that broke through the dark was from the truck's headlights.

"You must be tired, Cody." Fiona said, her voice low enough not to wake the boys. "Is your friend's house nearby?"

"It's only about ten miles more." Cody glanced over at her. It was too dark to see Fiona's face clearly but he didn't doubt she was tired. By his own choice, he wasn't used to having company while on the road. Solitude on the open road gave him time to mentally prepare for competition before he arrived at an event. It surprised him just how much he'd enjoyed having Fiona and the boys along for the ride, although a part of him knew he'd have to work twice as hard to stay focused and in the zone when it came time to compete. "I bet you're tired."

"I am. I had no idea how exhausting it is to sit still for so long." She shifted in her seat. "But I'm not complaining. I can't, not after the boys were so well-behaved today."

Cody smiled. "They were, weren't they? But you get a good deal of the credit for keeping them distracted."

They didn't speak again until Cody pulled the truck up in front of the house where they were going to spend the night. A buddy of his, who'd already arrived in Tucson, had offered Cody the use of his house and stable overnight. It was an offer he'd gladly accepted. He cut the engine, hopped out of the truck, and came around to open Fiona's door. "Here, let me help you. It's dark." He held out his hand and felt a surge of a mingled affection and desire as she slipped her hand into his. For the love of Texas, he was in over his head. "Watch your step."

Despite the warning, her foot missed the running board and she pitched forward with a startled cry. Cody reached out, slipped his free arm around her waist and pulled her close to him. "I got you." He lowered her so that her feet touched the gravel drive but he didn't loosen his hold on her. "You okay?"

Fiona looked up at him and nodded, although she didn't say anything. She didn't pull away from him either. Her hands were braced against his chest. Could she feel his heart hammering in his chest? There was just enough light coming from the cab that he could see her features in spite of the dark. He dropped his eyes to her lips. At that moment he wanted nothing more in the whole world than to kiss her.

And he would have too, if his horse hadn't kicked the back of the trailer to signal her impatience at being kept waiting. "Hold on, Chica, I'm coming." He loosened his hold on Fiona and took a step backwards. "I've got to see to getting her fed."

"Of course." Her voice was slightly breathless. "Should I wait here with the boys?"

"No, I'll carry them in first." He opened the rear passenger door and reached under the seat for his flashlight. He handed it to her. "There's a key under the doormat, think you can find it?"

She laughed. "Gee, I don't know, Cody, that sounds like a pretty high tech security system but I'll try to crack it."

He grinned. Again. He'd never known a woman who made him smile as much as Fiona did. "What can I say? It's a free place to sleep." He scooped up a still-sleeping Brian and took a groggy Mitchell by the hand. "Lead on."

Once the boys were settled in one of the guest rooms, Cody slipped out of the house so he could see to his horse. He was grateful for the cool night air as he led the mare down to the barn. He was equally grateful for the time away from Fiona. "She does a number on me, Chica," he whispered as he stroked her velvety muzzle. "She's turning my world upside down."

The buckskin, however, appeared far more interested in the feed bucket than in Cody's confession. He rubbed her neck affectionately as she ate. Horses he understood. Women, not so much. He took his time giving the mare a thorough brushing but after he'd stretched every task out as long as humanly possible, he knew he couldn't put off going back up to the house any longer. "What am I so afraid of?"

But he knew exactly what scared him. "What am I going to do after she leaves?" He hoisted himself up onto the wooden railing and sat with his legs dangling into Chica's stall. "She's beautiful, funny, smart, and nice. Like, really good-hearted nice. But she throws me way off my game, you know?"

The horse lifted her head and stared at him as if to say, 'Don't know, don't care'.

Cody grinned. "Got it, you want your beauty sleep." He jumped down and gave her one last affectionate pat. "See you in the morning, Chica girl." With one last check that the mare had everything she needed for the night, he secured the stall door. "You can stop worrying about me now. I'll watch my step with Fiona."

"WATCH WHERE YOU'RE STEPPING," Fiona called down to Cody as she clung to the saddle's horn. "There might be a snake somewhere." She shifted from side to side but there was no getting comfortable. "Can I get off now?"

The amused twinkle in Cody's eye when he looked up at her would have normally caused Fiona to smile. But panic, being what it was, kept her from appreciating any humor in the situation. Why had she agreed to mount this beast? She felt far too high off the ground for her comfort. Which was ironic considering that she, as a fairy god-mother, had spent more than her fair share of time with her feet far off the ground. But this was different. This was scary. Down-right unnatural.

"You volunteered, Fiona," he reminded her.

"Correction, I volunteered to help you get ready to hit the road. Not to sacrifice myself. Big difference."

Cody turned and began to walk backwards, all the while holding onto Chica's reins. "We put in a long day yesterday and we've still got to log more than three hundred miles to reach Tucson. That's a long time to have my girl cooped up."

By his girl, Fiona knew he must mean his horse, but the idea of sitting in the truck for another five hours didn't sit well with her either. However, she'd choose a motorized vehicle over equine transportation any day of the week. Make that every day of the week. "Shouldn't you turn around so you can see where you're going?"

Cody laughed. "We're in a round pen. Just what are you worried that I'm going to run into?" He turned his attention to his nephews who were perched on the railing. "Can you guys give some encouragement to Miss Fiona?"

"You're doing great, Miss Fiona," Brian hollered.

"Yeah, maybe you should try trotting now," Mitchell added.

"No, cantering is better." Brian stood on the rail and flapped his arms. "It's like flying."

Shows what little the child knew. Flying was a thousand times safer. Fiona forced herself to breath in and out before responding. "Walking is fine, thank you very much."

But Cody apparently didn't agree. "Whoa," he instructed the mare to stop. "Let's let her run. I'll come up with you."

Before she could protest, Cody's hand closed around her ankle. She watched in shock as he removed her boot from the stirrup.

"Sit still," he commanded as he slid his foot into the stirrup and swung himself up behind her. He slipped one arm around her waist and pulled her close up against him. "Relax, Fiona, I've got you."

He did have her, right in his arms, and that was precisely the problem. The proximity was intoxicating. Every single nerve in her body was on high alert. "I don't think this is a good idea. What if we hurt your horse?"

"Not possible." With his free hand he took the reins from her and made what sounded to her like a clicking sound with his tongue. Chica began to trot. Cody's breath was warm against Fiona's cheek. "Lean back into me and just relax. Nothing bad will happen to you, I promise."

Fiona closed her eyes and did as he suggested. Being in Cody's arms made her feel a thousand times safer than when she was alone. His body was lean and muscular but his arm that held her close was surprisingly gentle. She exhaled, glad to be able to breathe easily again.

"You're doing great," Cody said, his mouth only inches from her ear. "We're going to go a little faster so Chica can stretch her legs. But don't be afraid, I've got you and I'm not going to let you go. Okay?"

Fiona opened her eyes and nodded. She bit the inside of her cheek as Cody urged the horse to a canter. She was going to act brave if it killed her. Which, she realized after a few rings around the pen, it wasn't going to do. Far from it. As Chica continued to move, Fiona's body fell into a steady rhythmic movement that felt like she was connected to the horse. Connected to Cody. The morning sun touched her skin the same way the moment touched her heart. She wished their ride never had to end.

"UNCLE CODY, can I ask you something?"

Cody stopped brushing Chica and looked over at his nephew. Mitchell sat up on the stall's ledge, watching him groom the mare. Aside from his short legs swinging from side to side, he'd been remarkably still. Judging by his furrowed brow, his mind had been hard at work sorting something out. "You can ask me anything, buddy. What's up?"

"It's about Miss Fiona."

Cody's eyebrows rose. That wasn't what he was expecting to hear. "What about her?"

Mitchell cocked his head to the side. "Why do you act so different around her?"

"Different how?" He began to brush

Chica again, as much to get the job done as
to have some place to look other than his
nephew's curious face.

"Oh, you know. Mushy different."

"I don't know what 'mushy different'
means."

Mitchell sighed. "Brian and I know you
like Miss Fiona."

"Yes, I do like her. She's a very nice lady.
You guys like her too."

"Are you in love with Miss Fiona?"

Cody froze. Somehow, Mitchell's words
bypassed his head and went straight to his
heart. Was that how he felt? No. Of course
not. A man couldn't just fall in love with a
woman he'd met only a few days ago, no
matter how beautiful she was. No matter
how kind or funny she was either. That was
ludicrous. He turned to stare up at his
nephew but he couldn't force himself to
outright deny it.

"Just what I thought." Mitchell shook his
head ruefully. "You've got it bad."

And then Cody knew without a shadow
of a doubt that his nephew had just put
into words what he hadn't wanted to

admit to himself. He was in love with
Fiona.

"Uncle Cody? Hello?" Mitchell waved his
hands above his head. "Are you going to tell
her?"

His response was immediate and emphatic. "No, because there's nothing to tell
anyone, little man. Now let's put Chica out
in the pen while we get the truck packed up.
We've got to hit the road soon so we'll be in
Tucson before it's dark." He led the mare out
of the stall, pausing only to reach up and lift
Mitchell down.

"So you're going to deny your feelings?"

"You've been watching too much daytime television," he sidestepped the question. "We're done with this conversation,
got it?"

Mitchell held fast to Cody's hand as they
made their way out of the barn. "But I can
prove that you love her, you know."

Cody closed the gate behind his horse
and then knelt down so he could look his
nephew straight in the eye. "There's nothing
to prove." He hated to flat-out lie but he had

to draw the line somewhere. "Now, I really need your help getting your brother and Miss Fiona ready to go. So, please run up the house and tell them that anyone who wants to hitch a ride to Tucson needs to be by the truck in fifteen minutes. Can you do that?"

Mitchell nodded. "That's easy."

Cody stood. "Go on, the clock's ticking."

But not ten minutes passed before Cody heard a blood chilling scream. He dropped the pitchfork he'd been using to muck out the stall and ran out of the barn. Brian was running down from the main house as if the devil himself was on his heels. Cody ran toward him and scooped him up. "What's wrong? What happened?" He waited impatiently while the boy struggled to catch his breath. "Are you hurt?"

"No. It's not me," Brian managed between gulps of air. "It's Miss Fiona. She-"

But Cody didn't need to hear another word. He set Brian on the ground and ran toward the house. His heart hammered in his chest and fear made his boots feel as if they were made of lead. The thought of harm coming to Fiona was like a hand clawing at his throat.

He was twenty feet from the porch when Mitchell barreled out of the house, the screen door slamming shut behind him. But before he could call out to the boy, Cody's right boot heel caught on something and he pitched forward onto the grass. As he hit the ground, white pain exploded in his ankle and radiated through his body. Just as he would if he'd been thrown from a bucking horse, he rolled onto his side and tried to scramble to his feet but his right ankle wouldn't take his weight and he went down again.

"Mitchell," he called to his nephew, who remained on the front porch as if rooted, "what happened to Fiona? Where is she?" He ground his teeth together as he managed to get to his feet. He hopped over to the porch, lunging at the railing for support. "Answer me, is Fiona okay?"

Mitchell nodded but didn't speak, which only frightened Cody more. He hopped over to the stairs and managed to use his upper body strength and one leg to climb them. He gave his nephew's shoulder a gentle shake. "Tell me what happened."

But instead of answering, Mitchell pulled away, ran past him down the stairs and tore down to the barn.

"Fiona?" Cody called out, his voice nearly impossible to hear for the sound of his heartbeat thundering in his ears. Ignoring the waves of pain that rolled over him, he hopped over to the screen door. "Fiona?" he shouted. "Where are you?" But still there was no answer. He yanked the door open and collided straight into Fiona. He wrapped his arms around her, partially to keep from falling but just as much to keep her safe. "Are you okay?"

She didn't pull out of his arms but she leaned back so that she could look up at him. "I'm fine. What's going on?"

"You're okay?" he repeated, hardly daring to believe she was when he'd been so terrified she was injured. He held her closer still and buried his face in her hair, his relief so intense that he couldn't put together a coherent sentence.

"Of course, I'm fine." She pushed against

him. "Cody, look at me. What on earth is going on?"

Cody stared down at her. He didn't know what was going on, but he didn't care. Nothing mattered except that she was safe. And then, without giving himself a moment to talk himself out of it, he did what he'd wanted to do from the moment he'd first seen her. He kissed her.

9

F iona could never have imagined the sensation of pure bliss that was Cody's kiss. It was a moment she never wanted to end but all too soon Cody pulled back. For a long moment they stared at each other. Only a very telling silence spoke, and it told her everything she had been trying to ignore. But there was no ignoring her response to Cody's kiss.

"Are you sure you're okay?" he asked, his voice low and husky.

Okay? That was hardly the word to describe how she felt but she nodded. "What's going on here? I mean, with the boys screaming and you so worried?" To better see his face, she took a step backward, out of his embrace. Only then did she notice him the way he immediately reached out to lean against the wall for support. The grimace of pain on his face answered her unspoken question. She slipped an arm around his waist. "Lean on me."

"I'm okay."

"Bull." Fiona pulled him toward her and away from the wall. "Let's get you to the couch."

She heard the sharp hiss of his breath as he hopped on one leg toward the couch. Why had he been so scared about her when he was the one who was hurt? She eased him onto the couch. "What happened?"

Cody pointed to his right foot. "I need to get my boot off before the swelling gets worse."

Fiona pushed aside a litany of questions. The tightness in Cody's voice meant she needed to help first and quiz him later. As gingerly as she was able, she pushed the leg of his jeans up and delicately slipped off his boot. But cowboy boots weren't dainty slippers and it took a fair bit of pulling before she was able to get it off. Cody remained silent but the way he gripped the sofa cushions told her that her ministrations hurt him.

She rolled down his sock and saw that he was right. His ankle was already visibly starting to swell. "Let me get some ice." In the kitchen she threw some ice cubes in a kitchen towel and returned to place it over his ankle. "We need to find a doctor."

He shook his head. "No doctor."

She stared at him. "Why ever not? You're hurt."

"I don't run to a doctor every time I feel a twinge."

A twinge? She glanced down at his foot. Blue, green and purple were already rioting to see which would be the dominant color. "How do you know your ankle isn't broken?"

His smile was tight. "I've cracked enough bones to know when something is broken."

"Oh, I get it." Fiona plopped down next to him, angled so she could see his face. "This is a macho cowboy thing, right?"

"It's not a macho thing." Cody leaned

back and closed his eyes. "But you're not going to turn it into a sissy thing either."

Fiona counted to ten. Twice. "Cody, we need to get you some help."

He opened his eyes and turned his head to look her straight in the eye. "If you want to help, go round up those two little rascals for me. They're probably hiding in the barn."

But they weren't. Fiona found them sitting on the porch steps, both so quiet and contrite that she knew they were at the bottom of whatever had happened. "Alright, guys, let's go." She held open the screen door. "Your uncle wants to talk to you."

Like lambs to the slaughter, they filed into the living room.

"What happened to your leg?" Brian asked.

"You tell me," Cody shot back. "Start from the beginning."

"Well...," Mitchell managed to drag the word out for a good five seconds longer than necessary. "It's hard to explain."

"Try."

The brothers exchanged a quick glance.

"Remember what we were talking about in the barn?" Mitchell asked.

Cody's eyes widened. "What does that have to do with this?"

"I told you I could prove that you-"

"Stop." Cody frowned. "You've got to be kidding me. The two of you are unbelievable."

Fiona was lost, as in middle of the woods, wandering for days, lost. "I don't understand."

Cody shot a warning glance at the boys before looking at her. "Never mind. The boys and I will hash it out later. The important thing is that you're not hurt."

She laid a hand on his arm. "But you are."

"I'll live."

Technically, he was right. Fiona knew a sprained ankle probably never killed anyone but it definitely threw a crimp in their plans. "So what do we do now?"

Cody shifted again, trying in vain to get comfortable. "I need your help."

Every time he moved, every time he grimaced, Fiona felt a sympathetic stab of pain. She wished she'd been the one to fall.

"Of course, I'll do anything you need me to."

"I need you to load up Chica for me so we can get on the road."

Fiona stared at him as he were speaking Swahili. "What?"

"Uncle Cody said that he wants you to load his horse into the trailer," Brian translated.

"I know what he said," Fiona assured the boy. She turned to Cody. "First of all, that's insane. But let's just assume that I could manage it, then what? How are we going to get back to Texas?"

"The same way we're getting to Tucson. We're going to drive."

Her brain registered the defiant, challenging tone of his words even if what he said made no sense. "But you can't drive with your ankle like that."

"No, but you can."

Ah, but there he was wrong. She could sooner fly them to Tucson than get them there in the truck. "I don't know how to drive."

It was Cody's turn to stare at her, which

he did, his expression incredulous. "You're
kidding, right?"

She shook her head. She'd never learned.
Why bother when gold sparkles and a flick
of the wrist could get the job done far more
efficiently? She bit her lip and forced herself
to meet his gaze head on. "I'm sorry." And
she was, more than she would have thought
possible. She watched as a host of emotions
flitted across Cody's face. Shock, pain, disappointment, and worst of all, the realiza-
tion that if he didn't make it to Tucson, he'd
lose his sponsorship opportunity. It was a
blow that would bring any man to his
knees.

An uncomfortable silence filled the
room as the clock ticked away several long
minutes. Fiona willed away the tears that
pricked the back of her eyes. Cody's kiss
had taken her to a height she never could
have dreamt of but watching him absorb the
enormity of his loss was a low that she
didn't know even existed.

She reached for his hand. As his fingers
closed around hers, he gave her hand a gentle, reassuring squeeze. The generosity in

that gesture touched her heart like nothing ever had. "I'm sorry."

"We'll be okay."

Fiona wiped away a tear. "I'd give anything to take this away-" but then she stopped speaking. Anything. She'd give anything. She rose to her feet. "Wait, here. Promise you won't move?"

Cody nodded, his brown knit into a puzzled expression. "Where are you going?"

But she didn't answer. Her packed bags were still in the bedroom. "I'll be right back." She headed down the hallway before the voice of reason could stop her. Her small Lucite wand was just where she'd carefully tucked it into her folded red sequin gown. She shook it and then held it up the light streaming in through the window. It had to be at least seven-eighths full.

Fiona closed her eyes and hugged it to her chest. She knew what she had to do.

IT TOOK every ounce of self-control Cody had to sit helplessly on the couch. If he

could have his way, he'd be outside kicking
the truck's tires. Hell, if life was the least bit
fair he'd be heading west toward the Arizona border. Disgusted, he grabbed the hat
off his head and threw it across the room.

"Uncle Cody?"

He groaned. The boys. Caught up between his pain and disappointment, he'd
momentarily forgotten they were there. He
leaned his head back and closed his eyes.
There was no way he was going to look at
those two little faces while he was still so
angry. He was a grown man and they were
small children. There was no way he was
going to speak a harsh word to either one of
them, no matter how hare-brained their
little scheme had been. "What is it,
Mitchell?"

"Are you hurt?"

Cody resisted the urge to swear. Instead,
he exhaled slowly. "My ankle is sprained but
I'll live." He opened his eyes and composed
his face to as neutral an expression as he
could manage before he looked at his nephews. Much as he expected, they stood stiffly
with their hands clasped in front of them as

if they were members of a boys chorus. "Come over here, both of you."

They hesitated only a moment before they crossed the room.

"I'm sorry," Mitchell blurted out before Cody could say a word. "I just wanted to show you how much you love-"

Cody's hand shot up to forestall any incriminating words from being spoken. "Okay, we're going to set a few quick ground rules before Fiona gets back in the room." He lowered his voice. "Rule number one, no more using the 'L' word."

The boys exchanged puzzled glances.

"Love," Cody whispered. "That also means no more 'mushy' talk."

Brian turned to his brother. "What is he talking about?"

"You know," Mitchell puckered his lips and made kissing sounds.

Cody rolled his eyes. "Guys, get serious. No more." He fixed a hard stare on Brian and then an even harder one on Mitchell. "No more. Got it?" He pointed to his ankle. "I know this was an accident and I'm not mad. But I'm as serious as a southern

twister in summer that you have to behave.
No more trying to prove anything. In fact,
no more doing anything other than being
the helpful, polite, well-behaved little men
that your mom and dad are raising you to
be. Agreed?"

His nephews nodded their agreement.

"I'm back." Fiona came to sit next to him.
She leaned over and examined his ankle.
"How bad is it?"

Cody ignored the way his heart did a flip
flop in his chest. He wanted to believe it was
in reaction to the throbbing pain radiating
from his ankle but he knew better. "I've had
a lot worse. But I've come up with a plan.
Mitchell, run out to the utility room and
bring me one of the brooms."

"We can clean up later," Fiona said. "First,
I want to talk about your ankle."

Cody lowered his leg to the floor. "We
can talk in the truck. Right now I have to
get my horse loaded up."

Mitchell arrived with the broom just as
Fiona was in the middle of a vehement
protest.

"Thanks, buddy." Cody took the broom

and used it to hoist himself to his feet. It was a pathetic excuse for a makeshift crutch but it would at least help him keep some of his weight off of his right ankle as he loaded Chica into the trailer. "Let's go."

Fiona shot to her feet and stood in front of him. "Are you insane? You can't hobble around on a broom, and you certainly can't drive with your ankle in this condition. Sit back down."

Cody stared down at her. Her brown eyes sparkled with indignation. Under other circumstances he would have been amused, and certainly distracted, by her fiery opposition but not now, not here. Momentum was what he needed, not protests. "Look, I understand that you haven't spent any time on the rodeo circuit but let me assure you that crying over every little ache, pain, or sprain is not how it works."

"Oh, is that in the cowboy creed?" Fiona put her hands on her hips but she didn't budge. "Or have you fallen off a horse and hit your head so many times in the last few years that you've lost the ability to be reasonable?"

"You do fall a lot, don't you, Uncle Cody?"

Cody ignored Brian. Instead, he kept his eyes locked on Fiona's. In a battle of the wills, she certainly didn't think she could take him? "I don't compete for a couple of days yet. That's plenty of time for the swelling to go down."

"What about the driving?"

Lord, but she was stubborn. But so was he. "I can use my left foot and there's a little thing called cruise control that works wonders once we're on the highway." He used the broom to hobble to the side and would have moved past her but she put a restraining hand on his chest.

"Not so fast, cowboy."

"We can argue or we can get on the road." He had to fight to keep from grimacing as his ankle protested even the slightest movement. "I vote for the road."

"Consider yourself vetoed."

And then, in a move so swift and daring that he didn't see it coming, Fiona grabbed the broom out of his hand, tossed it out of his reach, and pushed him back down on the couch.

"Wait." She held up a hand. "Just hear me out. Please."

It was the 'please' that did him in, darn her. She was completely irresistible even if she was being insanely bossy. He nodded. "You have two minutes."

"No deal. I need twenty."

Cody started to protest but Fiona placed a finger over his lips.

"Just listen." She took a small, folded white towel that she'd brought into the room earlier and held it up. "I've made a poultice from some herbs that I always keep with me. All I'm asking is that you let me try it for twenty minutes." Without waiting for him to agree, she gently pulled his jeans leg up and wrapped it around his ankle.

"This is crazy," he protested, although the cold texture felt good against his skin.

"Have you ever used a poultice on a horse?" she demanded. "I bet you have."

He nodded, reluctant to concede the point.

"Then not another word." She stood.

"Don't move. Don't talk. Don't even think, if you can help it. The boys and I will be outside." With that order issued, she shepherded his nephews out the door.

Cody cursed under his breath but did as he was told. He closed his eyes. If nothing else, he could have a twenty minute cat nap before pronouncing this a total waste of time. But it didn't take even a few minutes before he knew something was happening. His pain level didn't just drop, it plummeted. He wiggled his toes but didn't feel so much as a twinge of pain. He flexed his heel but still nothing hurt. He pressed his fingers against his ankle. Still nothing. It wasn't that it was numb. It was normal.

Although there was no way that twenty minutes had passed, he removed the poultice and lowered his leg to the floor. Emboldened he pushed himself to the edge of the couch and, putting all of his weight on his left leg, he stood. He shifted his weight so that it was evenly distributed.

And felt absolutely no pain. None.

He whirled around as he heard the

screen door open. His eyes met Fiona's curious gaze.

"Unbelievable." He took a step toward her, hardly able to believe that his ankle could take his weight. It felt better than it had this morning. He took several more steps toward her. "Fiona, what have you done to me?"

10

Fiona's heart soared when she saw Cody walk without wincing. Her gold glitter had worked its magic. She resisted the urge to clap her hands together like a small child who'd just been awarded the grand prize. Instead, she cocked her head to the side and smiled playfully. "Now who wants to sit around and talk?"

Cody's answering grin, and the relief that practically radiated from him, made her decision to tap into her precious supply of glitter worth it.

Within the half-hour they had packed up, loaded Chica into the horse trailer, and were on I-10 west headed for the Arizona border.

Within twenty-four hours, while sitting in the stands at the rodeo grounds, Fiona knew that she was in terrible trouble. The ride into Tucson had been wonderful, Cody felt in top shape, the boys had been absolute angels, and Cody's cowboy buddies had been warm and welcoming. Cody himself had been kind, attentive, sweet...the perfect gentleman. These had been the best few days of her life. And she'd never been more miserable.

She gazed around the rodeo grounds, her eyes and ears registering a myriad of sights and sounds. There were families, cowboys, groups of friends, animals all existing in harmony, all gathered together to celebrate a sport that was more American than baseball. This was Cody's world, every bit as much, or even more than the ranch back in Texas was. This was his past, and his future.

Fiona closed her eyes and struggled to conjure up an image of Piccadilly Circus. Leicester Square. Buckingham Palace for crying out loud. But she came up with nothing. And that was a sign. A sign it was time for her to go.

How could she have lost all connection to her dream life in just a few days? No, this was insanity. Her arrival in Texas, trip through New Mexico, and now her time in Arizona was nothing but a massive distraction from what she really wanted. It had to stop.

She knew just who to call.

"Liam, I need your help," she spoke in a low whisper into her cell phone. "Is there any way you can come here? Please."

"Turn around."

Fiona did and nearly jumped out of skin to see he was standing right behind her. "Liam!"

He shoved his phone into his pocket and leaned in to kiss her cheek. Fiona took a quick step back and looked around.

"Oh, sorry, is your cowboy around?" Liam didn't try to hide his amusement. "I don't want to cramp your style."

"Don't be silly, and don't call him my cowboy." Fiona took Liam by the elbow and guided him to an area of the bleachers that were relatively empty. "Thank you for coming so quickly," she said after they sat.

Liam smiled. "You need me, we're here."

"We?" This was going to take some getting used to. She glanced around. "Tessa's here?"

"She said she wanted to come and see what it is about cowboys that make so many mortal women weak in the knees, or something like that." He patted her shoulder. "But I'm here for you so tell me what's going on. Where's Cody?"

"He wanted his nephews to try mutton busting."

Liam laughed loudly enough that several spectators turned to look at them. "I love it. You sound like a proper cowgirl. You look like one too." He studied her red leather boots. "I bet you'd like a pair of those covered in gold glitter, wouldn't you?"

Fiona groaned. "Don't talk to me about gold glitter."

"It sounds like I got here just in time, judging by the look on your face. What do you need?"

"Get me out of here."

"No." He stood.

Fiona pulled him back down. He'd never denied her a single request in all the years they'd worked together. Why was he starting now? "Don't leave. Please."

He shook his head, his expression sympathetic. "I can't help you with this. It's between you and Cody. But I understand how scared you are."

"I'm not scared."

His eyebrows rose. "Aren't you?"

Her eyes filled with tears. She shook her head but couldn't manage to speak. She'd never been able to lie to Liam. She wiped away her tears.

Liam reached into his pocket and handed her a neatly folded white cotton handkerchief.

She laughed through her tears. "Thank you." She dabbed her eyes. "A gentleman with a handkerchief for a damsel in distress. Such an old-fashioned notion."

"You know, Fiona, some of the best things in life never go out of style. Like good manners, and like love."

She stiffened. "Who's talking about love?"

"That's why I'm here, so let's not pretend we both don't know that." His gaze was probing. "Matters of the heart don't usually go according to a master plan. Falling for someone who comes from a different world than the one you live in can really shake you up."

Fiona nodded. "I can't believe any of this is real. Is it some kind of test?"

"Test?"

She searched his face for a sign that he was being coy but she couldn't see any evidence of it. "I thought perhaps you were testing my resolve to see if I really wanted to go to London."

"Do you?"

"Yes. Of course I do. It's not like I have a real choice to make here."

Liam's smile was kind. "You make whatever decision you need to, and I'll support you totally. But you owe it to yourself to at least be honest when you make your choice."

She nodded, her throat was tight with unshed tears.

Liam placed an arm around her shoulders. He didn't say anything. He didn't have to. He'd always understood her a heartbeat before she understood herself.

"Now," he said after several long moments, "I'm going in search of my wife before she decides to trade me in for a cowboy." He stood and drew her to her feet. He squeezed her hands. "And you have two little boys and one grown man down there that want you to be with them. That's where you belong."

"Thank you doesn't seem like enough." She laid a hand over her heart. "I'm so lucky to call you friend."

"Right back at you. It's our life's work to make other people's wishes come true, but that doesn't mean that our wishes can't come true too." And then he was gone, taking the bleachers two at a time until he disappeared out of sight.

Fiona watched him go with more than a little regret. He made everything sound so easy, as if she should know where she belonged. In London? Or with Cody? But it wasn't clear.

Not to her.

"HOW CAN I EVER THANK YOU?" Cody held Fiona in his arms, swaying in time to the music. He'd felt like a shy school boy when he'd asked Fiona if she'd like to attend the annual Barn Dance with him. The feel of her this close to him was as near to heaven as he'd ever imagined he was going to get. Her head lay on his shoulder as if they'd been custom made for each other.

"Your ankle doesn't hurt?"

"I've never felt better." Those were the truest words he'd ever spoken and he wasn't just referring to his ankle. "Are you going to tell me how you made my sprain disappear?"

She lifted her head and looked him square in the eye. "Nope. It's an old family secret so don't ask again."

"Yes, ma'am." He tightened his hold on her. "But I owe you, remember that."

Fiona laid her head back on his shoulder without responding, which struck him as odd. She'd been quiet all evening. Preoccupied? Worried? He couldn't tell. But maybe it was just the newness of the rodeo circuit. The horses, the crowds, the hectic energy of the holding areas, arena, the excitement and anticipation in the air; it was home away from home to him. But he could see where it might overwhelm someone new to it. "You're not worried about the boys are you?"

She laughed. "I'm more worried about your brave soul of a friend who volunteered to watch them. I don't think he or his wife will ever be the same again."

Cody grinned. "This evening will probably put them off having kids for awhile."

"You can't fool me." Fiona looked up at him. "You were about to burst from pride when Mitchell managed to stay on the back of that sheep a full four seconds. Admit it."

"Okay, yeah, I'm proud." They twirled around the dance floor in silence for a few moments. "It's special to see the boys experience a piece of my world."

He felt Fiona stiffen in his arms. "What's wrong?" But right in the middle of the dance floor wasn't the place for her to confide in him. He led her off the dance floor and out of a set of double doors to an outdoor patio. He stopped when they were in a quiet corner. "What is it?"

She shook her head but wouldn't look at him.

"Hey," he placed a finger under her chin and lifted it so he could look into her eyes. "Fiona, I want you to know that you can say anything to me." He cupped her face in his hands and traced her cheekbones with his thumbs. "Anything." He watched as her eyes grew moist.

"Can we talk about it later, Cody? Please."

"Of course." He leaned down and kissed her forehead. "Consider it a standing offer."

"Thank you." Her voice was barely above a whisper.

He took a step back and held out his hand to her. When she took a hold of it, he felt a rush of warmth straight to his heart. "I think we'd better call it an evening."

"Right, you've got your big ride tomorrow."

He nodded. He did need to get some rest and shift into competition mode but that wasn't the main reason he'd suggested they head back to the hotel. The truth was that if he spent so much as another moment with her, he wasn't going to be able to trust himself to remain a gentleman. He wanted to spend forever with her. And as crazy as that made him, he was going to tell her tomorrow.

Right after his ride.

11

"Boys, look. There's your uncle." Fiona pointed to where Cody stood in the midst of a group of cowboys. The clothes he wore, faded blue Levi's, a crisp white cotton shirt, black boots and a black cowboy hat, made him virtually undistinguishable from the other competitors. He wore his competitor number on the back of shirt but she didn't need that to pick him out of the crowd. Her eyes went straight to him as if he were the only man around. To her he was.

"Look, he's waving to us," Mitchell cried. Both boys jumped to their feet and waved their arms wildly. Fiona waved along with them, her face stretching into a huge smile when Cody tipped his hat in her direction. When he laid his hand over his heart, she did the same, and for a single magical moment it was as if they were the only two people in the world.

After the national anthem, the first event of the day was team roping. Much to her surprise, she enjoyed it immensely. Between the beautiful breeze, sunshine, and the blue sky, Fiona decided that February in Arizona was a small slice of heaven. The second event was tie-down roping and watching it gave Fiona a newfound appreciation for the teamwork between a cowboy and his horse. Between the novelty of watching new events, the gorgeous weather, and the boys' good company, she was able to keep her anxiety about watching Cody compete at bay.

"And now, Ladies and Gents, it's time for the competition that wears and tears at a cowboy's body more than any other. That's right, it's time for the bareback bronc riding event." The team of announcers both had mesmerizing voices that went a long way to keeping Fiona interested. She sat on the edge of her seat.

"Our first competitor is twenty-two year Tanner Bradshaw from Bismarck, North Dakota. How about we show Tanner a warm Tucson welcome before he rides?"

The crowd responded with enthusiastic cheers as the chute burst open. Fiona watched in shock as the horse bucked so high and so hard that it hardly seemed to have its hooves on the ground for three of the eight second ride. She held her breath until the two pickup men got close enough to carry the rider off.

She sat back in her seat, her heart hammering. "What went wrong?" she asked Mitchell. "Why did the horse go crazy like that?"

The boys exchanged puzzled glances. "The horse didn't go crazy. That was a good ride," Mitchell explained. "It just didn't like the flank strap." He pointed to the horse who was trotting out of the arena. "See how calm it is now?"

Fiona watched the horse exit through the gate before glancing around at the other spectators who filled the stands. No one looked particularly disturbed by the fact that a horse had bucked so furiously that the cowboy on his back looked like a rag doll trapped in the jaws of an angry dog. And Cody was going to do this? The thought turned her stomach.

"So now we just need to hope that your uncle gets a really quiet, calm horse."

"No!" Brian jumped to his feet. "That's not what we want."

"Why ever not?"

Mitchell frowned at his little brother. "Sit down and let me explain this." He turned to Fiona. "Both the cowboy and the horse get a score based on how they per-form. So we want Uncle Cody to get a horse that bucks hard and high."

"And what does your uncle have to do? Just hold on?"

Mitchell nodded. "Yes, with one hand. The other he has to keep in the air." He shrugged. "That's pretty much it."

Except that wasn't it because the next

cowboy came out of the bucking chute on a horse that looked every bit as wild as the first, yet the buzzer sounded half way through his ride. "Alright, Ladies and Gents, let's hear it for Sawyer Hale from Stillwater, Oklahoma. He'll be heading home with nothing but the memory of an appreciative Arizona audience."

Fiona looked at Mitchell. "What just happened?"

"He didn't mark out," he said with all the aplomb of a seasoned rodeo veteran.

"English, please."

Mitchell leaned in closer as if to answer discretely and save her the embarrassment of anyone overhearing her naive question. "He's supposed to keep his spurs above the horse's shoulders when he comes out of the chute, at least until the horse's feet hit the ground for the first time."

Fiona stared at him. "You're a pretty clever little guy to know all of this."

Mitchell shrugged, a half smile on his lips. "I have my moments."

Fiona laughed and ruffled his hair affectionately. "Yes, you do." She turned to

Brian. "Doesn't watching this make you nervous?"

"Not really. None of those horses weigh anything close to what a bull does. Some of them can weigh two thousand pounds. Now that would hurt if one kicked you, wouldn't it?"

Fiona nodded, but she left unsaid that a bucking horse could do plenty of harm to a person who wasn't wearing either a helmet or a suit of body armor. Clearly, the boys were proud of their uncle and if they were too young to be terrified by what he was doing, she wasn't about to enlighten them.

The wait for Cody to ride was excruciating. Her heart was in her throat each time a competitor rode. When Cody's turn came, Fiona had to force herself to breathe.

When the chute opened and the announcer began commentating on Cody's ride, she prayed as fervently as she ever had for the seconds to tick by without incident. But by the end of the third second, Fiona knew something was wrong. Whether it was her gut instinct or the slight hesitation in the announcer's narration, she didn't know. She jumped to her feet but couldn't tell what wasn't right, other than that the horse was bucking awfully close to the railing.

"What's wrong?" she asked aloud, but the boys were too fixated on watching the ride to answer. However, a man sitting in front of her turned around, his face grim.

"That rider's going to have to get off that horse now or else he's likely to get pinned against the chute, which makes it easy for the horse to kick the life out of him." He shook his head. "He should just let go and forfeit the ride."

Transfixed, Fiona stared in horror as Cody held on. The sound of the horse's hooves slamming into the metal barrier echoed through the open air arena. As if through an echo chamber, she could hear the indecision in the announcers' voices as they tried to describe a ride gone very wrong. Fiona glanced at the clock. How long could eight seconds possibly last?

As if in answer to her question, the buzzer sounded. Along with everyone around her, she stood and watched in horror as Cody was trapped on the bucking horse. There was no room for him to jump off. The horse's bucking intensified as if it knew its eight seconds were up and there was still a human on its back. A flurry of activity ensued around the gate, voices rose, and the pickup men worked to entice the horse away from the railings. There was no way they could remove the flank strap until the horse moved, but it only continued to furiously throw Cody's body against the metal siding.

She felt Brian tug on her hand. "Miss Fiona, what's happening?"

But she couldn't respond. She couldn't move. She could barely breathe. She closed her eyes against the horror of what was happening but she opened them again as a collective horrified gasp rippled through the arena. She strained to see through the commotion but she couldn't see Cody's white shirt. He was down, between the horse and barrier.

"Fiona," a voice next to her called.

She whirled around. It was Liam. His

grave expression told her that Cody's world had just forever changed.

CODY STRUGGLED to open his eyes but his eyelids, as heavy as steel, wouldn't cooperate. He needed to move, wanted to move, but he couldn't. Not a muscle. Breathe. He could breathe. Barely. His chest was heavy. Why weren't his eyes opening? Trying to think was like slogging through waist deep mud. An image of Fiona and the boys flitted across his mind but he couldn't catch it before it was gone. Why didn't anything hurt?

FIONA SAT on a hard plastic chair in the furthest corner of the hospital waiting room. She wrapped her arms around her waist but even then she couldn't quit shaking. Cody. Cody. It was as if her mind couldn't let go of his name, as if repeating it endlessly would keep him with her.

She'd reached the ambulance just as

they'd loaded the stretcher onto it. There'd been too many paramedics for her to be able to touch Cody but she had been close enough to be frightened by how still and lifeless his body was. Only after they slammed the ambulance's back doors shut did anyone notice she was there. A member of the rodeo committee had offered her a ride to the hospital. She'd nodded dumbly and followed him. He was there now, wearing dusty boots, his hat in his lap, in a chair several rows away. Close enough that she knew he was there but far enough away that she could have her privacy. But she could feel his eyes on her. His pity wrapped itself around her as if it were a blanket draped around her shoulders.

But he wasn't the man she needed with her while she waited for Cody to come out of surgery. Where was Liam? He'd never failed to appear when she needed his counsel. Not ever. Did that mean that there wasn't anything that they could do? No. No. That wasn't it. That couldn't be true. She wouldn't let it be true.

She closed her eyes and immediately saw

a vision of Cody standing in the rodeo arena. His clean, crisp white shirt was in sharp contrast to the dirt and dust around him. He was looking at her, a telling smile on his face. He tipped his hat in her direction right before he touched his heart. And then he faded away.

12

So this was hell.

Fiona hadn't expected there to be fluorescent lights, but then she hadn't really ever put too much thought into it. She was a fairy godmother. Her specialty was wish fulfillment, making dreams come true, not watching nightmares come to life.

And yet, here she was, on the front line of hopelessness.

"Ms. Cantrell?" The doctor's voice pierced through the distraction that fogged her mind. "You're waiting for news about Cody Proctor?"

She nodded. His expression held more

sympathy than she could bear. She wanted to see relief in his eyes, but there wasn't any.

"Are you here alone?"

She could only stare at him. It was too hard to talk. Even nodding was an effort too great to make.

"Actually, she's not alone. I'm waiting with her."

Startled, she turned around. It was Tessa. She was dressed in a black pinstripe suit and skirt more suitable for the boardroom than the waiting room. "Tessa, what are you doing here?"

"Obviously, I'm here to wait with you. There are also vultures circling and I'll take care of them in a minute. But first let's hear what the doctor has to say." She put a hand under Fiona's elbow and turned her around to face him.

Fiona never would have thought she'd be grateful to see Liam's wife but she felt a sudden surge of strength. "When can I see Cody?"

The doctor ran a hand over his tired face. "First things first. The patient made it through surgery."

The way he proclaimed this as news rather than a given sent a chill straight through Fiona. It's likely her knees would have given out from under her if Tessa hadn't literally been holding her up.

"What happens next?" Tessa asked, her voice crisp and detached. "What do we need to know?"

"Let's have a seat." He led them over to a semi-private seating area. "Look, I'll be very clear with you that we didn't expect the patient to survive surgery. He's suffered extensive internal bleeding, not to mention several broken bones. Our main concern, however, is twofold." He paused.

"Tell me," Fiona said.

He nodded. "Okay, the chance of paralysis is extremely high."

"And?"

"We're going to have to wait to give you a definitive diagnosis, but you need to understand that your friend has suffered a traumatic brain injury." He looked between the two women as if to assess their ability to read between the lines. "Frankly, from the blows he received to his head, I can't imagine that he will be the same man you knew if he wakes up."

If. If. If. Those two letters ripped through Fiona like a hot knife. She uttered a small cry and sagged against Tessa.

"I'm sorry." He stood. "We'll keep you up-dated as often as we can but it's going to be touch and go for quite awhile. We can talk in much greater detail after we've done more tests and after you've had a chance to digest this."

Fiona didn't even try to hide her despair. She let Tessa envelop her into a hug while she cried. Sobbed. Despaired. She didn't know where the line was between anything any longer.

After Fiona cried all the tears she was able, Tessa wiped her face with a tissue. "Let's get you cleaned up so you can get in there to see your cowboy."

"We forgot to ask if I could see him," she protested.

Tessa lifted one eyebrow. "I didn't forget. We didn't ask because we'll do what we want. You do want to see Cody, don't you?"

Fiona nodded.

Tessa's voice was unusually gentle. "Are you prepared for what you're going to see?"

"I can handle it."

Tessa smiled her approval. "Good girl. Now, go wash your face and compose yourself while I scope out the nurse's station. Unfortunately, my magic is useless to help Cody but I can at least guarantee that no one will bother you."

Fiona stood and held her purse against her chest. "But my magic will work, won't it? Did Liam say anything?"

Tessa stood and laid a hand on her shoulder. "He said there were no guarantees but you could try and see if you could perhaps alleviate a little suffering."

Try? That was it? Try? She closed her eyes.

Tessa snapped her fingers in front of Fiona's face.

Fiona's eyes flew open.

"You need to be strong for Cody. It's what you do when you love someone." She gave Fiona a gentle push toward the ladies room. "I want you back here within three minutes and I expect you to be a warrior. Now go."

And so Fiona went. She leaned over the sink and splashed cold water on her face several times. After she'd blotted her face with a paper towel, she stared at her reflection. It was hard to recognize herself, she looked like a frightened shell of the woman she'd been twenty-four hours ago. She heard Tessa's words in her mind. Be a warrior. She squared her shoulders and took a deep breath. She could do this. She could be strong. For Cody.

WHEN SHE CAME out of the ladies room, Fiona stopped short. Tessa was in the midst of what appeared to be a heated discussion with two men. Based on their attire, she doubted they were doctors or hospital administrators. Although they wore business suits, they also wore boots and bolo ties. They also carried brief cases. Tessa also carried one now. Fiona frowned. What was going on?

"Ah, there she is now." Tessa waved for her to join them. "Ms. Cantrell, I've tried to tell these gentlemen that you and I are already in negotiations regarding Cody Proctor's next contract." Her gaze was pointed and intense. "Perhaps you could confirm that so we can get back to our business."

What on earth was going on? Something was, but her mind was so numb with worry that she couldn't put two and two together. Fiona joined the group. "What's going on here?"

Tessa spoke first. "These two gentlemen claim they had a meeting with your client."

Her client? Was she talking about Cody? And then it dawned on her what Tessa wanted her to understand. These were the vultures. Fiona met Tessa's gaze and nodded imperceptibly. She would follow Tessa's lead because it was obvious that she had an agenda.

"I don't think this is the right time." Fiona looked from one man to the other. "Or the right place to discuss business."

The taller of the two men cleared his

throat. "We actually came to express our condolences."

Fiona bristled. Her look must have expressed her outrage because the second man quickly tried to cover for his associate.

"What we actually came to do was express our concern for Mr. Proctor's welfare. We witnessed the beating that he took and wanted to wish him well during his recovery."

Fiona was grateful that Tessa jumped right in.

"What these two gentlemen are trying to say is that they want to release Mr. Proctor from any responsibility to their company." Tessa reached into her briefcase and pulled out a folder. "Which gives me the floor. We're prepared to make a very generous offer to your client now that their offer is off the table."

"What company did you say you represented?" the first man asked.

Tessa raised an eyebrow. "I didn't say. My business isn't with you, it's with Ms. Cantrell. So, if you two would excuse us please?"

Neither man moved. "Have you spoken with Mr. Proctor's physicians?" one asked.

"Just a moment," Tessa interjected. "You can't come in here with the intent to drop Mr. Proctor from your list of potential endorsement clients and then try to muscle in on my deal." She handed the folder to Fiona. "I'll wait while you take a look at our offer."

"Now?" Fiona asked. Surely Tessa didn't expect her to stay out here and play along with whatever was going on. She wanted to see Cody.

"Absolutely," Tessa said. "After what happened today, your client is going to be considered a rodeo hero. I mean, after what that horse did to him, it's going to seem like a miracle when he rides back into that arena later in the season. Mr. Proctor is going to represent the epitome of true grit and the American spirit." She smiled at the men who considered her to be their competition. "But I've said enough. If you couldn't get here fast enough to hear what the doctors said, well, that's your loss, isn't it?" She pointed to the folder that Fiona held. "Go ahead, take a look at that now. I want to ink a deal today."

Fiona opened the folder and gasped at the amount of money she saw on the bottom line.

Her reaction spurred the two men into action.

"Now, hold on a moment, Ms. Cantrell. We expressed an interest in signing a contract with Mr. Proctor many weeks ago. I feel that it's only fair that you consider our offer first."

"But are you prepared to sign a contract today?" Tessa demanded. "Because I am."

"Of course, we are." One of the men took a folder from his briefcase and held it out to Fiona. "We'll accept your verbal agreement with a hand shake today."

Wearying of continuing the charade, Fiona forced herself to keep her heartbreak from showing. She opened the folder and a quick glance told her just why Cody had been so intent on scoring a win today. She closed the folder and held out her hand to each of the men in turn. It took a herculean effort but she acted the part of Cody's business manager for the few minutes they loitered in the waiting area.

As soon as the elevator doors closed behind them, she sank into a chair. "Oh, Tessa,
I can't think anymore." She buried her head
in her hands. It wasn't time to cry now. If
she gave in to the sobs that threatened to
engulf her she wouldn't be able to stop.

"They're gone now."

Fiona turned to look at her.

"It's unfortunate that we had to waste
time doing that," Tessa said. "But it was necessary in order to protect Cody's interests."

Fiona nodded. "Thank you."

"Don't thank me. There's precious little I
can do to be of true help."

"You're here."

The words hung between them for several long moments.

"Go on, Fiona. Go in and see Cody. I'll
make sure that the coast stays clear."

13

When Fiona pushed open the door to the ICU unit she immediately saw that Tessa had been true to her word. There wasn't a nurse in sight. As if by instinct, she was drawn to the room where they'd taken Cody. Between the bandages and the tubing attached to him, he was virtually unrecognizable. The room was cold, clinical, and filled with machines that made frightening noises as they worked to keep Cody alive.

She closed her eyes against the stillness that surrounded her. Hadn't the day started with blue skies and sunshine? Laughter and anticipation? Hopes, dreams, and togetherness?

She approached the bed. A silent sob tore through her when she reached Cody's side. His form was lifeless, his eyes closed, his dark eyelashes the only color on his bandaged face. With a tentative hand she reached out to touch a small part of his hand that wasn't bandaged. She stroked his skin as gently as a butterfly might land on a rose.

"I'm here, Cody." She wiped away the tears that streamed freely down her face with her free hand. "I need you to hold on. Don't let go. We need you." She took a deep shuddering breath. "I need you."

'Be a warrior', Tessa's words echoed in her mind.

It was time for battle.

Fiona set her purse on a chair and dug through it until her fingers closed around her wand. A quick measurement told her what she already knew, there wasn't enough glitter to begin to heal Cody but she had to try something. How much time she had was completely dependent on how long Tessa's magic held out. But how to start? Where to start? According to what the doctor had said, Cody likely faced both paralysis and brain damage. It was the ultimate impossible choice. Did she try to heal his body or his mind? Cody was young and strong, and his livelihood came from riding. But that was only because of his keen intelligence and his choices as to how to live his life. She thought of the joy in his eyes when he talked about riding. She blew out a long breath and then inhaled, seeking courage and guidance.

She would start with his spirit.

A TINY RAY of light pierced through the darkness. Cody wanted to turn toward it, to exchange the cold for the warmth, but he was unable to move. However, he was able to feel. He felt fear. Dread. And a desperate longing to break out of the blackness that he was submerged in. For all that he was worth, with all the strength he had, he struggled to focus on the sliver of light.

FIONA SLIPPED out of the ICU unit and into the hallway. She looked around but Tessa was nowhere in sight.

But her husband was.

"Liam." Fiona sank into the nearest chair, too relieved to cross the room to where he stood. He was here. That had to be a positive sign. Didn't it? "You came," she said, when he sat beside her.

He nodded. "Tessa's with the boys." He attempted a half-hearted smile. "I think they've just met their match."

"Are they okay?"

"They will be. Children have a remarkable way of reframing events with enough guidance from caring adults."

Fiona recognized the fairy godparent doublespeak for what it was, an admission that he'd done his best to alter their memories so they'd avoid the traumatic memory of what they'd witnessed today. There was much good that fairy godparents could do, but there were limitations. "I feel so powerless."

"Fiona," he said, his voice gentle, "We're

not angels. Our powers are limited to granting wishes."

"Don't talk to me about limitations, Liam Kennedy. And don't you dare try to prepare me for the worst because it's already happened." She grabbed ahold of his arm. "I need more gold glitter."

"You used everything you needed for London?"

"Forget London. That means nothing to me. I'm not going and I don't care about it." Her eyes pleaded with him to understand. "I need more glitter and I need you to get it for me. I'm begging you." She'd beg, she'd borrow, and she'd certainly steal. She'd do anything. "I know it will work, if I could just get enough. I felt Cody react to it."

Liam's eyes widened. "He responded?"

"No, not the way you're thinking. But his skin immediately absorbed the gold the second I applied it. That's a good sign, right?"

He remained silent.

"Look, Liam, I don't have time to be diplomatic about this. I need every single speck of glitter you can get for me. I will do anything, pay any price, for it. There's nothing I won't give to bring Cody back to us." She decided it was time to drive her point home. "You would do it for Tessa."

"You love him that much?"

She nodded, unable to speak. There were no words.

Liam stood and began to pace the length of the waiting area. It took every ounce of self control for her to sit quietly.

Liam returned to kneel beside her chair. He took one of her hands in his. "Of course, I'll give you everything I can spare. I've put the word out within the community and we both know that fairy godparents are nothing if not generous. But we also both know it's not enough." He held up a hand when she started to protest. "Don't talk. I need you to hear me out."

She nodded.

"There's only one way that you can get enough to possibly reach Cody."

"I'll do anything," she repeated.

"I can't believe it's come to this." He

shook his head. "I don't even want to say it out loud."

"Tell me."

He stood and drew her to her feet. He held her hands in his. "Your only option is to request a one-time disbursement of gold glitter. You know what that means?"

Her mind raced to process his words. "It means that I'd no longer be a fairy godmother."

He nodded. "It's not a decision you should make in haste."

"I want to do it." She didn't need time to think. "Now."

The silence in the waiting area surrounded them while they both waited for the other to speak. But Fiona wasn't going to back down. Or change her mind. She was ready to give up everything.

"There's one more thing you have to know before I can, in good conscience, let you go through with this." He gave her hands a gentle squeeze. "There were angels at the rodeo."

Fiona ignored the tears that pricked the back of her eyes. "They weren't there for

Cody." She shook her head. "Somebody else, but not him."

"He has to want to come back."

"He does."

Liam eyes were sad. "You're completely certain you're ready? This is an irrevocable decision."

She squared her shoulders. "We're wasting precious time."

"I'll go then." Liam drew her close and hugged her for a long moment before he reached into his pocket and handed her a vial of gold glitter. "I'll send more as I get it. I'd suggest you make yourself invisible because the mortals won't let you stay with him around the clock."

"Thank you, Liam." She held the glitter he'd given her next to her heart. "I know I can reach Cody."

———

CODY'S EYES went back and forth between the shaft of golden light and the stark white one. Both called to him. He struggled to make sense of them, the only thing he knew for sure was that either choice would be better than the darkness. His brain was exhausted, his spirit weak, but he knew it was time to make a choice. His eyes went back to the white one. Just looking at it filled him with relief. If he chose the white light, he wouldn't hurt anymore. It would keep him out of the pain's reach. And there was so much pain.

He looked at the gold light again. When he did, there wasn't the peace that the white promised him, but the gold warmed him straight through to his heart. It was as if it offered him a golden sword, one he could reach out and grasp so that he could fight his way through the pain.

He closed his eyes, too tired to think any longer.

"IT'S NOTHING SHORT OF A MIRACLE." A team of three doctors faced Bethany, Tessa and Liam, who stood on either side of Fiona. The lead doctor handed a chart to a nurse. "I can't even pretend to explain how Cody survived, let alone how his brain function is testing so high. None of us have ever seen anything like it."

Fiona glanced over at the bed where Cody slept. He slept a lot, which the doctors assured them was normal and necessary. They bandied the word 'total recovery' around in awed tones, which was the way mortals usually spoke of miracles. There was no more talk of paralysis. Fiona knew, even if they didn't just yet, that Cody's physical rehabilitation would be swift. His recovery would soon be complete, which meant it was time for her leave.

After the conference, Fiona pulled Bethany aside. "Can I have a moment alone with Cody? I want to say goodbye."

Bethany's shock was clear. "Where are you going? Wait, why are you going?" She reached out and grabbed Fiona's hand. "Cody's going to want to see you when he wakes up." Her eyes filled with tears. "You've been by his side from the start. We're all so beholden to you."

Which was exactly why Fiona had to leave before Cody woke up and heard from his family and the nursing staff about what he 'owed' her. She squeezed Bethany's hand and then pulled away gently. "No one is beholden to me, certainly not Cody. I was here with him because I wanted to be." She took a deep steadying breath. "He's going to be fine now. And I am so, so happy about that."

"Fiona, I know you love my brother." Bethany's voice was gentle. "Does he feel the same way about you?"

Fiona shook her head. "I don't know." She thought of the way his kiss had made her feel. It hurt to remember. It seemed so long ago that they'd set out for Tucson, far longer than the five weeks it'd been. "But I do know I have to go."

When Bethany finally left them alone, Fiona took Cody's hand in hers. His skin was warm and his color was good. It just looked as if he were asleep. "Oh, Cody, I'm so happy that you're going to be okay." She brushed a gentle kiss across his knuckles. "Be happy." It was hard for her to find words powerful enough to express the way her heart felt. "Be safe. But most of all be happy."

She leaned forward and kissed his cheek. "I love you."

And then she turned and left the hospital, knowing full well that her heart remained behind with the cowboy who'd stolen it.

14

"So, I think that covers everything for today." Fiona slipped the agenda and meeting minutes into her binder. She smiled at the assembled group of volunteers that were the lifeblood of her new life's work, a nonprofit she'd named 'Magic Wand Ranch'. "I think we're in good shape for our first event next month. The budget looks healthy and our plans solid. I want you all to know how deeply grateful I am, and the families we're helping will be as well."

After a motion to adjourn was made and seconded, those assembled filtered out of Fiona's house and, one by one, began to depart. Just as she was saying goodbye to the last member of the group, she saw an unfamiliar pickup truck pull into the driveway. She held a hand up to block out the sun's glare but the only thing she could make out clearly was that it was hauling a horse trailer.

"Are we expecting someone?" she asked her office manager.

"The only thing I could think of is that it's the horse that someone wanted to donate. They could be delivering it a few days early. You want me to hang around?"

Fiona shook her head. "Nope, I can handle it. You go get your weekend started and I'll see you on Monday."

Fiona leaned against the front porch pillar and watched as the driver pulled the truck aside so that her manager could pass by before it continued up the long gravel drive. She never imagined that in six short months she'd have had as much success getting her non-profit off the ground as she'd had. Not that she'd done it alone. The generous response from her new neighbors and friends in Las Cruces had gone a long way to making her feel that she could make her venture successful. But the true kudos went to her former colleagues at Fairy Godmother, Inc. who had showered Fiona with an outpouring of kindness and support after she'd turned in her wand. She'd lost her magic, lost her wings, and lost her heart to Cody, but she'd been given the great gift of knowing he'd recovered. Despite the massive upheaval to her life, she'd not regretted her choice for a single second. Now that she had a new mission in life to bring terminally ill children and their families to the ranch for a week of rest and relaxation, she was busy. Busy enough that she only thought of Cody every other second.

As the truck grew closer she saw that it was a pearly white color and clearly showroom new. The driver was the only person in the cab but he was wearing a cowboy hat that hid his face. But it was the lettering on the truck doors and trailer that caught her attention. The words 'Magic Wand Ranch' were spelled out in sparkly gold letters. A delighted grin stretched across Fiona's face.

But who on earth had arranged such an amazing surprise?

She walked down the porch steps as the truck drew to a stop. She went over to the passenger door and ran her fingers reverently over the glittery letters.

The driver's side door opened and she looked up to see who had brought her such an unexpected gift. When the driver took off his hat and met her eyes, Fiona gasped.

Cody.

She couldn't move but her eyes greedily drank in every detail of his appearance. He looked healthy, strong, and more perfect than she could have ever hoped for. When he came around the front of the truck, she was delighted to see that he walked without even the suggestion of a limp.

Cody set his hat on the hood of the truck and held his arms open wide.

Fiona didn't hesitate.

He closed his arms around her and swung her around twice before he set her gently down, but he didn't release his hold on her hands. "Hello, Fiona."

"Cody, what are you doing here?" Was he

really here? She hadn't even dared dream
that he'd come find her.

"I brought you a gift. Two gifts, actually."
He motioned to the horse trailer with his
head. "The truck and also the world's most
gentle Palomino mare. I thought your
guests might like riding Glitter Girl."

"Glitter Girl?"

He smiled, his eyes twinkling. "I named
her after you."

"I don't understand."

Instead of answering, he twirled her
around so that her back was to him. He ran
his hands lightly over her shoulders where
her wings used to be. He sucked in his
breath. "So it's true."

She whirled back around and took a step
back. "What are you talking about?"

"Fiona, I know." His smile was tender.
"Your friends told me about your life before we met. I know what you gave up
for me."

She shook her head. There was no way
that Liam would ever betray her trust that
way. "My friends?"

"It wasn't Liam. I couldn't get anything

out of him, but his wife sang like a caged canary."

Fiona reeled from the shock of Tessa's betrayal. She'd never for a moment thought she'd see Cody again, let alone stand and face him knowing that he knew her secret. She felt exposed, vulnerable, in a way she'd never imagined possible.

"Fiona." Cody gently took her hands in his, "I owe you my life."

"No." She shook her head. "Your medical team was amazing. I didn't do anything."

"Yes, you did. You were the golden light. You were what I came back for."

This was what she'd dreaded, the reason she'd left before he regained consciousness. "I did what I had to do and I'm happier than I can say to see you looking so perfectly healthy and strong."

"I know I don't have the right to ask this of you, but I need a few more things from you." His eyes searched hers before he continued speaking. "Will you hear me out?"

She nodded. She hadn't a single idea what he was going to say but if it meant she had one more moment to listen to his voice, and to look into his eyes before he left, she'd take it.

"I sold the ranch."

Her eyes widened. This was the last thing she'd expected to hear. "Why?"

His eyes didn't leave hers. "I was going to go to London."

Fiona wanted to laugh and cry at the same time but she struggled to maintain her composure. "Why didn't you?"

"Because the girl I love wasn't there." He grinned. "It took me awhile but I tracked her down, sold everything, packed up my horse and here I am."

And here he was. This had to be a dream. But if it was, she didn't want to wake up. "So, what are your plans now?"

Cody grinned. "Well, that all depends on you. I'll always be a cowboy, but my bronc riding days are over. I have a pretty lucrative deal thanks to you-"

"No, that was all Tessa."

"Well, I'm grateful to have enough money to start over. I wondered if you'd hired a ranch manager yet?"

Her mind scrambled to understand what

he was asking of her. "You want to stay here?"

He nodded. "But only if I can stay forever."

Oh, what that one little word did to her heart, but she needed to be sure she understood him. "Forever?"

"Do you remember that day at the rodeo, right before the competition started? When I tipped my hat-"

"And touched your heart."

"And touched my heart," he repeated. "That was the moment when I knew that I wanted to spend the rest of my life with you."

She barely dared hope that she understood him. "Cody, I have to know. You aren't here because you feel like you owe me something?"

He reached out and caressed her cheek. "I do owe you my life, but I'd already decided before I rode that day that I wanted to marry you. If you'll have me, that is. I don't have much of anything to offer but-"

Fiona didn't let him finish. She threw

herself into his arms and hugged him tightly to her.

He laughed. "Is that a yes?"

She nodded. "Yes, it's a yes." She smiled up at him through her tears.

When Cody lowered his lips to hers and kissed her, Fiona recognized their love for what it was.

Pure magic.

A NOTE FROM CAROLINE:

Thank you so much for reading *'Magic Wand Ranch'*. I had fun writing it and I hope you enjoyed reading it too. Please consider leaving a review on the site where you purchased this book. Please visit my website to join my newsletter list if you'd like to hear when I have a new release out or when I'm running a contest. Lastly, in case you aren't familiar with the story of how Liam and Tessa met, I'd encourage you to pick up a copy of *Witch Weigh*.